W9-BEQ-164

"Let's start again. Imagine you're in love with me," Mary ordered him.

Tyler blew out an irritable breath, but turned obediently back to study her.

She looked different tonight, he realized, looking at her properly for the first time. Her hair was a soft cloud around her face. She was wearing a floaty sort of skirt, and a top with a plunging neckline that emphasized her generous cleavage. Beneath it she wore a lacy camisole, the discreet glimpse of which hinted deliciously at hidden delights, and made Tyler's head spin suddenly with images of sexy lingerie and silk stockings.

He swallowed. "All right," he said. "I'm imagining."

The odd thing was that the more he looked at her, the more he *could* imagine it. Not the whole being in love thing, obviously, but it wasn't that difficult to imagine wanting to kiss her, wanting to discover if those lips were as sweet as they looked, wanting to unwrap that top and see what that lace was concealing.

"What am I supposed to say?" Tyler asked.

"Make me believe that you love me," she said.

Jessica Hart

Vibrant, fresh and cosmopolitan,
Jessica Hart creates stories bursting with
emotional warmth and sparkling romance!

Jessica Hart won the prestigious RITA®
Award for Best Traditional Romance 2005!

You'll love her sparkling stories—they are
the essence of feel-good romance!

Look out for Jessica's next story,
Barefoot Bride
Coming in March

JESSICA HART
Business Arrangement Bride

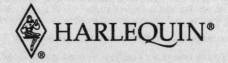

HARLEQUIN®

TORONTO • NEW YORK • LONDON
AMSTERDAM • PARIS • SYDNEY • HAMBURG
STOCKHOLM • ATHENS • TOKYO • MILAN • MADRID
PRAGUE • WARSAW • BUDAPEST • AUCKLAND

If you purchased this book without a cover you should be aware
that this book is stolen property. It was reported as "unsold and
destroyed" to the publisher, and neither the author nor the
publisher has received any payment for this "stripped book."

ISBN-13: 978-0-373-18263-3
ISBN-10:   0-373-18263-5

BUSINESS ARRANGEMENT BRIDE

First North American Publication 2006.

Copyright © 2006 by Jessica Hart.

All rights reserved. Except for use in any review, the reproduction or
utilization of this work in whole or in part in any form by any electronic,
mechanical or other means, now known or hereafter invented, including
xerography, photocopying and recording, or in any information storage
or retrieval system, is forbidden without the written permission of the
publisher, Harlequin Enterprises Limited, 225 Duncan Mill Road,
Don Mills, Ontario, Canada M3B 3K9.

All characters in this book have no existence outside the imagination of
the author and have no relation whatsoever to anyone bearing the same
name or names. They are not even distantly inspired by any individual
known or unknown to the author, and all incidents are pure invention.

This edition published by arrangement with Harlequin Books S.A.

® and TM are trademarks of the publisher. Trademarks indicated with
® are registered in the United States Patent and Trademark Office, the
Canadian Trade Marks Office and in other countries.

www.eHarlequin.com

Printed in U.S.A.

Jessica Hart was born in West Africa, and has suffered from itchy feet ever since, traveling and working around the world in a wide variety of interesting but very lowly jobs, all of which have provided inspiration to draw from when it comes to the settings and plots of her stories. Now she lives a rather more settled existence in York, where she has been able to pursue her interest in history, although she still yearns sometimes for wider horizons. If you'd like to know more about Jessica, visit her Web site, www.jessicahart.co.uk

CHAPTER ONE

WHERE had he seen her before?

Tyler watched the woman across the room as she smiled and shook hands with a group of men in suits. He had noticed her as soon as she arrived, and it had been bugging him ever since that he couldn't work out why she seemed so elusively familiar.

It wasn't as if she was the kind of woman who would normally catch his eye. Apart from that luminous smile, there was nothing remarkable about her at all. She had nondescript features and messy brown hair, and she was squeezed into a suit that was much too small for her. Stylish and beautiful she definitely wasn't.

And yet…there was *something* about her. Tyler couldn't put his finger on it and it was making him cross. He was a man who liked to know exactly what he was dealing with, and he was irritated by the fact that his gaze kept snagging on this very ordinary-looking woman who was taking not the slightest notice of *him*.

He had been watching her for nearly an hour as she circulated easily around the crowded room. She obviously had the ability to relate to people that he so conspicuously lacked, according to Julia, anyway.

'You're a lovely person, Ty,' his best friend's wife had told him with her usual candour, 'but honestly, you've got the social skills of a rhinoceros!'

Tyler scowled at the memory.

Unaware that his glower had caused several of the people around him to flinch visibly, he took a morose sip of champagne and surveyed the crowded foyer of his new building. He hated occasions like this. He couldn't be bothered with all the social chit-chat that woman seemed to be able to do so well, but his PR director had insisted that a reception to mark the opening of his controversial new headquarters would be politic. So now he was stuck here in a roomful of civic dignitaries and business-people, all of whom seemed to be hovering, hoping for a chance to ingratiate themselves, to lobby for his support for their pet schemes or to suggest mutually beneficial business opportunities. They all wanted to talk to him.

All except her.

She hadn't so much as glanced his way all evening.

Some councillor was boring on about the city's local transport plan, and Tyler let his gaze wander over the room once more, wondering how long it would be before he could decently leave. Why had he agreed to such a tedious PR exercise anyway?

Suddenly he realised that he couldn't see the woman any more, and he felt oddly jolted to have lost her. Frowning, he searched the crowd with hard eyes. Had she gone? Surely she would have—

Ah, there she was! She had found a quiet corner by herself and was easing off her high-heeled shoes. Tyler saw her grimace. Her feet were obviously killing her. If she had any sense she would go soon, and he would never find out who she was. The thought was oddly unsettling.

He could ask someone, he supposed, but the group around him were still droning on about Park and Ride schemes.

Or he could go over and ask her himself.

'Excuse me,' he said brusquely—who said he didn't have social skills?—and, leaving the rest of them in mid bus lane, as it were, he headed across the room towards her.

In her quiet corner near the lifts, Mary was surreptitiously wriggling the toes on her left foot and wishing she had the nerve to take off her right shoe as well.

The shoes had seemed a good idea when she'd put them on too. The news that Tyler Watts, the North's very own bad boy made good, was moving the headquarters of his phenomenally successful property company out of London and back to York had riveted the business community, while his construction of a cutting edge building on the river front had divided opinion across the city. It had outraged conservationists and delighted others who claimed it as stunning proof that the city could not only hold on to its historical heritage but also stake a claim as being at the forefront of architectural design in the twenty-first century.

Either way, the champagne reception to celebrate its opening was certain to be the networking opportunity of the year, and Mary was determined to make the most of it. She wouldn't be the only one lobbying for a contract with Watts Holdings, and she might make some useful contacts even if she didn't get the big one.

So she had chosen her outfit carefully. This was her first public outing as a professional woman since Bea's birth, and she wanted to look elegant and…well, professional. A smart suit and stylish shoes would create the perfect impression. Mary knew; she had read all the magazines.

Sadly, the magazines didn't tell you what to do when you realised, five minutes before you were due to go out, that you were a good two sizes larger than you had been the last time you put on your best suit. Nor did they remind you what agony it was standing around on high heels, and that was before you tried walking on what some bone-headed architect had decided was cutting edge flooring, apparently forgetting that a glassy sheen was more appropriate to an ice rink than an office building.

Mary sighed and switched shoes, giving her right foot a break. As so often in her life, she reflected glumly, there was a huge gap between imagination and reality. She had pictured herself charming the assembled employers of York, so impressing them with her professionalism that they were queuing up to get her to solve their recruitment problems, but it hadn't worked out like that. Oh, everyone had been very pleasant, but they had all wanted to talk about Tyler Watts, not business, and while no one had been rude enough to point out that her jacket was straining across her ample bust, no one had offered her any work either, and she had been burningly aware that professional was the last thing she had looked.

All she had got out of the evening was pinched toes and a sore back.

Mary took a slug of champagne, put down her glass and squeezed her poor foot back into its shoe. She would make one last effort to meet the Human Resources director of Watts Holdings, she decided, and then she would give up.

It was at that point that she detected a ripple of interest around her and looked up from her shoe to see none other than Tyler Watts bulldozing his way across the room, groups parting and stepping back sycophantically to make way for him.

Not that he noticed or acknowledged them, Mary noted sourly. That was typical of him. In her brief meetings with him in the past he had struck her as the most arrogant and ruthless person she had ever met and she was in no hurry to renew her acquaintance with him. She might want a contract with Watts Holdings, but she had no desire to deal with the man at the top, thank you very much.

Extraordinarily, he seemed to bо heading straight towards her. Mary glanced around her, in case there was someone interesting standing behind her shoulder, but she was momentarily isolated.

If she didn't do something about it sharpish, he would be on top of her and there would be no avoiding him.

Picking up her glass from the table beside her, Mary turned to slink behind the group on her left, but she was too hasty and hadn't reckoned on the slippery floor. The next thing she knew, one of her wretched heels was skidding out from beneath her and she pitched forwards.

There were indrawn breaths around her as everyone anticipated an almighty crash, but she never hit the floor. A hard hand caught her under her elbow, swivelling her up and round until she was upright once more. More or less upright, anyway. One of Mary's arms was still flailing madly as she tried to regain her balance, and the polished floor wasn't helping at all.

Mortified, she managed to stand on two feet once more. 'Thank you so—' she began breathlessly, and then the words died on her lips as she looked up and found herself staring into Tyler Watts's glacial blue eyes.

Her first thought was that he must have moved at the speed of light to reach her in time, her second was that he was incredibly strong. She was not exactly a lightweight, but he had caught her and hauled her upright with a single hand.

It was only then that she noticed the stain on the front of his shirt. Somehow, in all her skidding and flailing, she must have knocked the glass in his hand.

'I'm so sorry,' she said nervously.

She didn't want to be nervous, but there was something about Tyler Watts that made you feel edgy. You had to admit, the man had presence, and it wasn't anything to do with looks, although the dark, beetling brows and grim lines of his face were intimidating enough on their own. He exuded a restless, driven energy that reverberated around him and left people half thrilled, half mesmerised by a mixture of awe and apprehension when he was around.

Not a man you would choose to knock drink all over.

Good move, Mary, she thought with an inward sigh. She had thought her aching feet were the low point of the evening, but apparently not.

Tyler's fingers were still gripping her arm just above the elbow, but as Mary's eyes dropped to them he released her.

'Are you all right?' he asked brusquely.

'Yes, I'm fine. Thank you.' She managed a nervous laugh and resisted the urge to rub her skin where he had held her. Her whole arm was tingling and throbbing from his grip and it was making her feel a bit odd.

'This floor is lethal in heels,' she tried to explain in case he thought she'd been over-indulging in the free champagne. 'But that's trendy designers for you,' she said, conscious that she was babbling but too rattled by his nearness to think sensibly. 'What clot thought a floor like this would be a good idea?'

'That would be a clot like me,' said Tyler Watts with a sardonic look.

If a black hole had yawned at Mary's feet at that moment, she would gladly have jumped into it and disappeared. How could she have said anything so stupid? Criticising the design of the building that marked the culmination of a spectacularly successful career to a man whose business she desperately needed was *not* a good move.

'You've obviously never tried walking on it in high heels!' she said, deciding that her only option was to make a joke of it, but Tyler was unamused.

'The other women seem to be managing to stay upright,' he pointed out. 'Perhaps it's your shoes that are the problem, not my floor?'

They both looked down. The shoes were Mary's favourites—or had been until they had started hurting so vilely—and she had chosen them deliberately because they reminded her of her days in London when she had been slim—well, slimmer—and sharp and successful. They were black with white polka dots, so you could get away with wearing them with a suit, but the peep toes and floppy bow were fun when you didn't want to be *too* serious.

Maybe the heels *were* a bit high, Mary conceded to herself, but what kind of office floor was designed without stilettos in mind?

Tyler looked down at the shoes, noticing in passing that she had surprisingly nice legs, and shook his head at their impracticality.

'I suggest you wear something more sensible next time.'

Mary opened her mouth to say that being sensible was good advice coming from a man who had chosen a floor like an ice rink, but she managed to stop herself in time. She was supposed to be drumming up business, not alienating potential clients.

'I'll do that,' she said instead, and if there was a suspicion of gritted teeth about her smile, she didn't think Tyler Watts would notice.

She hadn't really wanted to talk to him but, since he was there, she had better make the most of the opportunity. Somehow she had to convince him that she was a competent businesswoman and not just a tactless idiot in silly shoes. If he were to be impressed enough to recommend her to his Human Resources director, her problems would be over.

Her most pressing ones, anyway.

Summoning a bright professional smile, Mary held out her hand. 'I'm Mary Thomas,' she said.

The name didn't ring a bell with Tyler, but then it wasn't a particularly memorable one. In fact, there was nothing particularly memorable about her now that he had a chance to study her more closely. She had beautiful skin and intelligent grey eyes, but her round face was quirky rather than pretty, with eyebrows that didn't quite match and features that all seemed to tilt upwards, giving her a humorous look.

None of which explained why she seemed so familiar.

Irritated by his inability to place her, Tyler took her hand and shook it. 'Tyler Watts,' he introduced himself briefly.

'I know,' said Mary, acutely aware of the feel of his fingers closing around hers and pulling her hand away rather sharply.

'You do?'

'Everybody knows who you are,' she told him, nodding around the crowded lobby. 'You're famous in York. Everyone here wants to talk to you and do business with the new expanded Watts Holdings.'

'Including you?' he asked.

'Including me,' Mary agreed. 'Except that I was hoping to meet Steven Halliday rather than you.'

The dark brows snapped together. 'What's wrong with me?' he demanded.

'There's nothing wrong with you,' said Mary hastily, more intimidated than she wanted to admit by his frown. 'I just thought it would be more appropriate to talk to Mr Halliday. I understand he's your Director of Human Resources?'

More appropriate and a lot easier. Mary didn't know what Steven Halliday was like, but he had to be a whole lot better to deal with than the glowering Tyler Watts, who famously gave his staff a mere thirty seconds to make their point. She would really rather talk to someone with a bit more patience, not to mention a few listening skills.

To someone who wouldn't insist on looming over her with that ferocious frown and those unnervingly pale, polar-blue eyes that seemed to bore into you. It was hard to keep your cool when faced with that mixture of arrogance, impatience and sheer force of personality.

'He is,' Tyler admitted grudgingly. 'What do you want to talk to him about?'

'I'm in recruitment.'

This was the perfect time to produce one of those cards she had had printed at such expense. Mary had been dishing them out all evening, though, and she just hoped that she had some left.

Digging around at the bottom of her bag—really, she *must* organise it—her fingers closed around a card just as the pressure of her hand snapped the fragile chain and the whole thing lurched downwards, spilling most of the contents over the floor, where they skidded merrily over the glossy surface.

Mary closed her eyes. Excellent. Fall over, knock drink over him, insult his design taste and tip her handbag all over the floor... Could she look any more of a fool, and in front of the man with the power to make or break her precious agency, too?

Pink with embarrassment and irritation with herself, she stooped to gather up keys and lipstick and business cards—there were plenty left, it appeared—plus a sundry collection of pens, safety pins, tissues, scraps of paper with scribbled lists, a couple of floppy disks, an emery board and a plastic baby spoon.

A biscuit left in an opened packet ended up at the tip of Tyler's perfectly polished shoe and Mary scrabbled to retrieve it. That explained all the crumbs in the bottom of her bag anyway. It must have been there for ages, and the wonder was that she hadn't eaten it.

Tyler bent and picked up a spare nappy, which he handed to Mary with an expressionless face.

'Thank you,' she muttered, shoving it into the bag along with the rest of the stuff and straightening.

She was amazed that he was still there, and

couldn't think why he hadn't walked off in disgust long ago. Why had he come over in the first place, in fact? she thought with a trace of resentment. She had been perfectly all right, minding her own business and not doing anything stupid, and then he had turned up and transformed her into a blithering idiot.

But Tyler showed no sign of walking off. He just stood there, looking daunting, and waited for her to explain what she was doing there.

Tyler was, in fact, bitterly regretting having come over to talk to her. He had moved instinctively to catch her when she'd fallen, not realising how heavy she would be, and he was lucky she hadn't taken him down with her. As it was, she had managed to knock the champagne he'd had in his free hand all over him. Always fastidious, Tyler was very conscious of the stain on his shirt and, as for his tie, it was probably ruined, he thought crossly.

Not content with that, she had criticised his floor, and he didn't take kindly to criticism from anyone, let alone someone who wore ridiculously inappropriate shoes and evidently possessed a handbag as messy as the rest of her. Everyone had turned to look as the contents scattered over the floor, and they had probably noticed him there too with a nappy—a nappy, of all things!—in his hand and a spreading stain on his shirt, and no doubt looking a fool.

If there was one thing Tyler hated, it was feeling ridiculous.

Actually, there were lots of things that he hated, but looking stupid had to be way up there at the top of his list.

He wished he had never been sucked into Mary Thomas's chaotic orbit, but now that he was here he couldn't think of a way to leave. If they'd been in a meeting, he could just have told her that her thirty seconds were up but, as it was, she was looking pink and flustered and he didn't feel able to turn on his heel and walk off, no matter how much he might want to.

'What sort of recruitment?' he asked after a moment, deciding to pretend that the whole bag incident had never happened.

Mary only just stopped herself from sighing in time. She had been willing him to make an excuse and leave, at which point she could have slunk off home and enjoyed her humiliation in comfort.

This was a fantastic opportunity for her. Half the room would give their eye teeth to be in her position, with Tyler Watts's apparently undivided attention. She should be making her pitch and sounding gung-ho, but it was hard when your feet were aching, your toes pinched, your jacket was gaping and you had just humiliated yourself three times in as many minutes in front of the man you had to try and impress, and when you would really much rather be stretched out on the sofa in front of the television with a cup of cocoa.

But lying on the sofa wouldn't get her agency off the ground. It wouldn't get her a home of her own, or make a new life for Bea.

Lying on the sofa wasn't an option.

Mary took a deep breath and, mentally squaring her shoulders, handed Tyler a business card and launched into her carefully prepared spiel.

'I understand you're expanding your operation in the north now that you're making York your head-quarters, so if you need people with accountancy, clerical, computer or secretarial skills, I hope you'll think of my agency. I can find you the best,' she told him with what she hoped was a confident smile.

'I don't deal with junior staffing decisions,' said Tyler, frowning down at her card.

'I'm aware of that, which is why I was hoping to meet Steven Halliday here.' Mary kept her voice even and hoped that she didn't sound as desperate as she felt. 'I have worked for Watts Holdings in the past myself, so I understand the company ethos and how it operates,' she went on. 'That's a huge advantage when it comes to finding suitable staff, as I'm sure you are aware.'

But Tyler wasn't listening. 'You've worked for me?' he said, a very faint light beginning to glimmer.

'It's nearly ten years ago now, so you won't remember me,' said Mary, a little unnerved by the way the pale, polar-blue eyes were suddenly alert as they rested on her face. 'I worked in Human Resources here in York. Guy Mann was director then.'

'Ah…!' Tyler let out a hiss of satisfaction. He had it now.

Mary Thomas… Of course.

'I do remember you,' he said slowly. 'You were the one who spilt coffee all over the conference table at some meeting.'

Of course, he *would* remember that. Mary bit her lip and averted her eyes from the stain on his shirt. 'I'm not usually that clumsy,' she said.

'And you stood up to me over that guy… What was his name?' Tyler clicked his fingers impatiently as if trying to conjure the name out of thin air.

'Paul Dobson,' Mary supplied, since there was no point in pretending she didn't know.

'Dobson…yes. You told me I was wrong.' He eyed her with new interest. Very few people dared to tell him he was wrong about anything.

It was all coming back. He could remember the shocked silence around the table as Mary Thomas had spoken out, the scorn in her voice, how taken aback they had all been, as if some gentle kitten had suddenly puffed up to twice its size and lashed out without warning.

'I hope I put it a bit more diplomatically than that,' said Mary, her heart sinking. He would never give her work if he associated her with trouble.

'There was no diplomacy about it,' said Tyler.

'You told me flat out that I was wrong and should be ashamed of myself.'

He had been furious at the time, Mary remembered, marvelling now that she had ever had the nerve, but when she risked a glance at him she was sure she detected a gleam of something that might even have been amusement in the chilly blue eyes. It had a startling effect, lightening the grimness of his features and making him seem suddenly much more approachable.

'You told *me* I was a bleeding heart,' she countered, emboldened.

'So you were,' he agreed. 'But a bleeding heart who got her own way, I seem to remember.'

Mary nodded. 'You were fair,' she acknowledged.

That was one thing you could say about Tyler Watts. He might be rude and impatient, and the most difficult and demanding of employers most of the time, but he was straight and he didn't ignore or manipulate facts that didn't suit him. Irritated he might have been, but he had listened to what she had had to say about Paul Dobson. The upshot had been a special inquiry, and Tyler had been prepared to reconsider his decision when he knew more.

Well, that explained why she had seemed so familiar, anyway. Tyler felt better. He didn't like being puzzled or uncertain. Having solved the mystery, he could move on, but he was remembering something the HR director had once told him:

'Mary Thomas may be young, but she's got an instinctive understanding of human relationships.'

And, if that were still so, maybe Mary Thomas could be of some use to him after all.

'Why did you leave Watts Holdings?' he asked her.

Mary, trying to relaunch into her sales pitch, was thrown by the abrupt question. 'I wanted to work in London,' she said, puzzled by his interest. 'I grew up in York and I was really lucky to get a job with you after I graduated, but after three years I was ready to spread my wings.'

'You could have got a job with us in London.'

He sounded almost peeved that she hadn't. She hadn't realised that joining Watts Holdings was supposed to be a lifetime commitment. Mind you, there had been some fanatically loyal members of staff who probably thought of it that way. There tended to be a very high turnover amongst the rest, though, most of whom were terrified of Tyler Watts. Mary had only managed to survive three years by not being important enough to have much to do with him.

Still, better not tell Tyler that. She had been tactless enough for one evening.

'I wanted to broaden my experience,' she said instead.

'Hmm.' Tyler's hard eyes studied her with such intentness that Mary began to feel uncomfortable. 'And now you're back in York?' he said.

'Yes. I've been back a few months now,' she told him, relieved that he seemed to be getting back to the business in hand, which was about winning some work.

'I've recently set up a recruitment agency,' she went on, ready to launch back into her spiel and wishing that her feet didn't hurt so much. 'I offer a complete headhunting service for junior staff. Companies tend to spend a lot of money recruiting senior members of staff and skimp on employees at lower grades, but it's a false economy in my view.

'A financial investment in finding exactly the right person, however lowly the job, pays dividends,' she said. 'If all your staff, from janitors to chief executives, are doing the job they're best suited to, your entire company will function more efficiently.'

Tyler was unimpressed. 'Sounds expensive,' he commented.

'It's more expensive than accepting anyone who happens to have the skills to do the job,' Mary agreed. 'But less expensive than realising you've appointed someone who doesn't fit into the team or who doesn't work effectively with their colleagues.'

She was beginning to perk up a bit now. Tyler's expression might be unresponsive, but at least he was listening. 'Before I look for the right person for you, I need to understand the company culture, and that means working very closely with your human resources department. It's important to know exactly what the job entails and what sort of personality would fit most comfortably into the existing team.

'I see my job less as matching skills and requirements, and more about forging successful human relationships,' she finished grandly. She always liked that bit.

Relationships, the dreaded R word! Tyler was sick of hearing about them. He had recently spent a weekend with his best friend and his wife, and Julia had spent her whole time banging on about 'relationships' and making free with her advice.

'For someone so clever at business, you're extraordinarily stupid when it comes to women,' she had told him bluntly. 'You've got no idea how to have a relationship.'

Tyler had been outraged. 'Of course I do! I've had loads of girlfriends.'

'Yes, and how many of them have lasted more than a few weeks? Those are encounters, Ty, not relationships!'

Tyler was fond of Julia in his own way, but her comments had caught him on the raw, especially after that reunion he had gone to with Mike where all his peers seemed to be measuring their success suddenly in terms of wives and children rather than share value or racehorses or fast cars.

'That's what being really successful is nowadays,' Mike had said, amused by Tyler's bafflement. 'You're going to have to get yourself a wife and family, Tyler, if you want to be the man who really does have it all!'

'And you won't be that until you learn how to have a relationship,' Julia added. 'If you want to be the best, Ty, you're going to have to get yourself a relationship coach.'

It was all rubbish, of course, but her words had rankled with Tyler. He liked being the best—*needed* to be the best, even—and he wasn't prepared to accept that there was anything he didn't do well, even something as unimportant as relationships. He didn't do failure, in any shape or form.

Now here was Mary Thomas going on about relationships too.

'What is it with all this relationship stuff nowadays?' he demanded truculently. 'Why is it no one can just do the job they're paid to do any more? Why do they all have to spend their time *forging relationships*?'

'Because unless they *do* form relationships, they won't work effectively,' said Mary, who was wishing Tyler Watts would stop talking and let her get out of these shoes. 'You know, it's not a big deal,' she told him when he made no effort either to move on or to hide his scepticism. 'It's not about hugging each other or sitting around chanting. It's just about understanding that different people have different approaches, different needs, different expectations. It's about being aware of other people, of what they do and how they do it.'

She attempted a smile, although they tended to be rather wasted on Tyler from what she could remember. 'Like any other relationship, in fact.'

To her surprise, an arrested expression sprang into the cold blue eyes that were boring in to her. 'Do you think you can teach that?'

'Teach what?'

'All that stuff you were just talking about…you know, understanding, being aware of people…' Tyler waved a dismissive hand, clearly unable to remember any other alien concepts.

'Of course,' said Mary, surprised.

This was one area she really did know about, thanks to Alan. He had been running a coaching course when she'd met him, and she had been bowled over by his psychological insights and grasp of the complexities of human relationships.

Of course, it hadn't helped when their own relationship had fallen apart, but that was experts for you.

'I've run a number of courses on workplace relationships in the past,' she went on, thinking there would be no harm in bigging herself up a little. 'It's an interesting area, and it's amazing what a difference tackling problems like this can make to a company's productivity.'

'Do you do other kinds of coaching?' Tyler asked.

'Yes.' Mary was really getting into her stride now. 'I can help people identify their goals at a personal level and work out a strategy to achieve them.'

Now she was talking his language. Tyler looked at her with approval. He might not have a clue about relationships, but he understood goals and strategies all right.

'In that case, I might have a job for you,' he said.

Mary was taken by surprise. 'I thought you weren't involved with staff recruitment?'

'This isn't about staffing,' he said. 'It's about me.'

'Oh?' said Mary, puzzled but polite.

'Yes.' Characteristically, Tyler went straight to the point. 'I want to get married.'

CHAPTER TWO

MARY laughed. 'Well, this is very sudden!' she said, entering into the spirit of the joke and pretending confusion. She pressed a hand to her throat as if to contain her palpitations. 'I don't know what to say. I had no idea you felt that way about me.'

'What?' Tyler stared at her.

'Still, it's a good offer,' she said, putting her head on one side as if giving it serious consideration. 'I'm thirty-five, and a girl my age can't be picking and choosing. I'm up for it if you are!'

Looking down into her face, Tyler realised with a mixture of incredulity and outrage that she was *laughing* at him. The grey eyes were alight and a smile was tugging at the corner of her wide mouth.

'I'm serious,' he said, glowering.

The smile was wiped off Mary's face and it was her turn to stare. 'I thought you were joking!'

'Do I look like the joking type?'

'Well, no, now you come to mention it, but... No, come on.' She laughed uncertainly. 'You *are* joking!'

'I can assure you,' said Tyler grimly, 'that I am not in a humorous mood.'

'But…you don't want to marry me, surely?'

His expression changed ludicrously. 'Good God, no!' he said, appalled at the misunderstanding. 'I don't want to marry *you.*'

Charming, thought Mary acidly. She knew that she wasn't beautiful and, OK, she was a bit overweight at the moment, but she wasn't *that* bad, and Tyler was no George Clooney, when it came down to it. He had no call to look as if he would rather pick up slugs than touch her.

'Well, you know,' she said, leaning forward confidentially, her smile a-glitter with defiance, 'that's what the princess in the fairy tale always says to the frog, and you know what happens to them!'

Tyler's fierce brows were drawn together in a ferocious scowl, and if Mary hadn't been so cross with him by this stage she would have been quailing in her heels. As it was, when he demanded, 'Do you want a job or not?' she only looked straight back at him.

'I'm not at all clear what this job of yours involves,' she said. 'Or, to put it another way, I haven't a clue what you're talking about!'

A passing waiter, seeing that they were without glasses, approached with a tray, only to falter as Tyler waved him away irritably, but as the man made to retreat Mary gave him her best smile.

'Thank you,' she said. 'I'd love one.'

Ignoring Tyler's glare, she helped herself to a glass of champagne. She didn't care what he thought anymore. It was late, she was tired, her feet hurt and she was fed up with Tyler Watts looming over her. She didn't know what he wanted, but it didn't sound like it was anything to do with recruitment, and that meant he was wasting her time.

'I think you'd better go back to the beginning,' she told him coolly and took a sip of champagne.

Tyler drew a deep breath and counted to ten. If he was the kind of man who was prepared to admit that he had made a mistake, he would have to accept that he might have made a big one in approaching Mary Thomas.

When the idea had first struck him, she had seemed ideal. She had been talking about coaching and he needed a coach. More to the point, he didn't want to spend time finding a suitable coach, and here was one, right in front of him and anxious for work, it seemed.

Her ordinariness had been appealing too, if he was honest. While accepting in principle the idea of a relationship coach—it was just one step in his strategy, after all—Tyler hadn't been looking forward to the prospect of discussing his private affairs with anyone too smart or sophisticated. He had every intention of remaining in control of the whole process, and Mary Thomas had looked suitably meek and deferential. All he wanted was for her to offer him a few pointers and then fade into the background.

But the closer he looked, the less ordinary she seemed. Take away that ill-fitting suit and those ridiculous shoes, and you would be left with a lush figure and an impression of warmth that made an intriguing contrast with the direct grey gaze and the slight edge to her voice. Mary Thomas, he had realised already, was not going to do meek or deferential.

It was annoying, Tyler admitted. He had decided that she was the person he needed, and once he had made up his mind he liked to go straight for what he wanted. His ability to focus on a goal and his refusal to be diverted had been the secret of his business success and he wasn't going to change a winning strategy now. He didn't have time for doubt or hesitation. He needed to get Mary Thomas on side, and get the job done.

'All right,' he said. 'I'll start again. I want a wife.'

There was a pause while Mary tried to work out what was going on. He sounded utterly clear and utterly serious but she couldn't see how this could be anything other than a very elaborate joke at her expense. People just didn't *say* things like 'I need a wife'.

Although, perhaps, people like Tyler Watts did.

'I think you've misunderstood what I do,' she said

after a moment. 'I'm not a dating agency. I can find you a secretary or a computer operator, but not a wife.'

And then she offered a smile, just in case he turned out to be joking after all.

Tyler looked down at the empty glass in his hand, made an irritated gesture and put it down. He was getting frustrated. Mary Thomas didn't seem to be taking this seriously at all.

'I don't want you to find me a wife,' he said in a taut voice. 'I'm just trying to explain. Getting married is my goal. I just need a bit of coaching to get there.'

'Coaching?' said Mary, trying to look willing but still confused about where she came into all this.

'Yes, you know…relationship coaching.'

Tyler couldn't quite hide his distaste of the term, although Mary wasn't sure whether it was relationship or coaching that was the problem for him. There was a very slight tinge of colour along his cheekbones and he looked faintly uncomfortable.

Mary's interest sharpened. The Tyler Wattses of this world would normally only discuss emotions if they were listed on the stock exchange, so it must be costing him a lot to even mention the word *relationship*, let alone with the implication that he needed some help on that front. Men like Tyler Watts didn't do asking for help any more than they did talking about their feelings. Things must be pretty bad.

She had only ever thought of Tyler as an employer, but of course he was a man too. And not an unattractive one, Mary had to admit. He projected such a forceful personality that it was hard to get past that and look at him properly, but if that cold blue stare didn't have you trapped like a rabbit stuck in headlights, it was possible to see that he had a face that was dark and strong rather than handsome.

The fierce brows, jutting nose and forceful jaw were familiar, of course, but she had never noticed his mouth before, she realised. It was rather a nice mouth too, now she came to look at it. They might be set in a stern line right now, but his lips looked cool and firm, and it would be interesting to see what they would be like if he smiled.

Or feel like if he kissed.

Sucking in an involuntary breath at the thought, Mary caught herself up sharply and stamped down firmly on the little tingle that was shivering its way down her spine.

What was she *thinking* of? This was *Tyler Watts*, of all people. He was a hard man, and she didn't envy the woman he was planning on marrying. It would be like cuddling up to a lump of granite.

On the other hand, she would know what it was like to kiss him.

Enough. Mary pulled her wayward thoughts sternly to order.

'Relationship coaching isn't really my field,' she said carefully. 'If you're having problems with your fiancée, there are plenty of organisations that offer counselling and will be able to help you. I could put you in touch with them, if you like.'

'I don't need *counselling*,' said Tyler, outraged at the very idea. This was all proving much more difficult to explain than he had anticipated. 'I haven't got any problems. I *haven't*!' he insisted crossly when Mary just looked at him.

'What does your fiancée think?' she asked.

'I haven't got a fiancée, that's the point,' he snapped, goaded by the needle in her voice.

'But you said you wanted to get married,' said Mary, puzzled.

'I do.'

'Then who do you want to marry?'

'Anyone—anyone except you,' he added hastily. '*Anyone?*'

'Well, not *any*one,' Tyler amended. 'Obviously I'd want my wife to be beautiful and intelligent and sophisticated, but the point is, I don't have anyone particular in mind yet.'

Incredible. He actually meant it, thought Mary. It was an oddly old-fashioned attitude for a man who had built this extraordinary twenty-first century building, but there wasn't so much as a glimmer of laughter in his voice, and she could only conclude that he was serious. Anyone would think he was some stiff-necked earl planning a marriage of convenience in a Regency romance.

'I'm sorry, but I still don't see where I come in,' she told him, looking around for somewhere to put her empty glass.

Tyler raked a hand through his hair in frustration. 'Look, finding a woman isn't a problem,' he said with unconscious arrogance.

Mary would have loved to have contradicted him, but she was afraid it was all too true. Tyler was in his early forties and had built his company up from nothing to be listed in the top hundred in the country. He was extremely wealthy, undoubtedly intelligent, apparently straight and even attractive if you liked the ruthless, hard-bitten type—and let's face it, lots of women did, even when the toughness wasn't accompanied by loads of dosh.

No, Mary could see that acquiring a girlfriend wouldn't be too difficult for Tyler.

'Then what *is* the problem?'

'Keeping her,' he said. 'I want to get married, but my relationships aren't lasting long enough to get engaged.'

'Maybe you just haven't met the right woman yet,' Mary suggested mildly, but he dismissed that idea.

'It's not that. No, there've been several suitable women, but I'm doing something wrong. That's where you come in.'

'I don't see how,' said Mary frankly.

'You said that you ran coaching courses where you helped people identify and achieve their goals.'

'Well, yes, but in a work context,' she said. 'I help people with their careers, not their love lives.'

Tyler brushed the distinction aside. 'It's the same process, surely? I've identified my goal—to get married. I need you to help me with my strategy.'

'Relationships aren't like business plans,' said Mary. 'You can't have a strategy for emotions!'

'Everything's a strategy,' said Tyler. He dug his hands into his pockets and hunched his shoulders. 'I'm obviously getting something wrong,' he conceded. 'You work out what that is and tell me what I should be doing instead. I apply what I've learnt to my next relationship, the relationship works, I get married and achieve my goal. That's strategy.'

Mary sighed. 'I can tell you now what you're getting wrong,' she said. 'Your attitude.'

'What's wrong with my attitude?'

'Relationships just don't work like that. I can understand wanting to get married, but first of all you need to fall in love and that's not something you can plan for. You can't predict when you're going to meet the right person. It's not like interviewing for a job, you know. Falling in love isn't about mugging up a few notes, drawing up a list of criteria and finding someone who more or less fits your requirements!'

That was exactly what Tyler had planned to do. 'I think you're over-romanticising,' he said stiffly.

'The goal here is to get married. It's not about falling in love.'

'But if you want to get married, that's exactly what it should be about,' said Mary, appalled.

'You don't really believe that love is the only reason people get married, do you?' he asked, raising his brows superciliously, and Mary lifted her chin.

'Yes, as a matter of fact, I do!'

'You're a romantic.' He didn't make it sound like a compliment. 'My own view of the world is a little more practical…perhaps realistic would be a better word,' he added after a moment's consideration.

'I'm prepared to accept that some people do indeed get married because they're *in love*, whatever that means,' he went on, putting sneery quotation marks around the words, 'but you're a fool if you think it's the only reason, or the only good reason. There are plenty of equally valid reasons to marry.'

'Like what?' she demanded, profoundly unconvinced.

'Like security…stability…comfort…fear of loneliness…financial incentives…status…convenience…'

'Oh, *please*!' Mary rolled her eyes. 'Marriages of convenience went out centuries ago!'

'I disagree,' said Tyler. 'I think the idea of settling into a routine where you don't have to think about making the effort to go out and impress someone new is very appealing for a lot of people. Knowing that there's someone else to do the cooking and cleaning, or change the plug, or pick up the dry-cleaning, is a lot more convenient than having to think about everything for yourself. I imagine there are a lot more happy marriages based on comfort and convenience than on bodice-ripping passion.'

Mary opened her mouth to disagree, then thought about her mother's second marriage. Her mother had been open about the fact that she was settling for comfort this time round, and she had been very happy with Bill. Until Bill had decided that comfort wasn't enough, of course, but that was another story.

'Perhaps,' she allowed, 'but I don't see you as someone who's short of comfort and security and all that stuff. You certainly don't have any financial incentive to get married! So why get married unless you are in love?'

'Because I've decided that's what I want to do,' said Tyler curtly. He didn't have to explain himself to Mary Thomas. 'You're not concerned with the goal, only with how to achieve it.'

Mary shook her head. 'I'm not concerned with any of it,' she corrected him. 'I'm sorry, but I can't help you. You're not talking about the kind of goals and strategies I want to be associated with.'

His brows drew together in the familiar frown at the flatness of her rejection. 'I thought you were looking for work?'

'Not that kind of work,' she said. 'Recruitment opportunities, yes.'

'And if I tell Steven Halliday I don't want your agency considered if any recruitment contracts come up?'

Mary's eyes narrowed dangerously. 'That's blackmail!' she said, and he shrugged.

'That's business. I want something from you, you want something for me. Why should I give you what you want if I don't get what I want in return?'

'That's not *business*,' said Mary, her voice shaking with fury. 'I'm offering you an excellent service. If you choose to use that service, you pay me for what I do. *That's* business.'

Tyler merely looked contemptuous. 'That's not the deal that's on offer here.'

'Then you can keep your deal! I may be desperate for work, but I'm not that desperate!'

'Sure? The recruitment contract will be a lucrative one.'

'I'm sure,' said Mary distinctly. She took a firmer grip of her bag and got ready to leave. 'You know, I'm not surprised that you have problems forming relationships if your first response to rejection is bullying and blackmail,' she told him, too angry by now to care about alienating him, his company or the entire business community if it came to that.

'What makes you think that I'd want to be involved in your pathetic strategies?' she went on in a scathing tone. 'I can think of better goals to work towards than seeing some poor woman trapped in a loveless marriage with someone so emotionally stunted! Frankly, the whole idea is offensive.'

A muscle was jumping furiously in Tyler's jaw and there was a dangerously white look around his mouth. It was some satisfaction to know that he was as angry as she was.

'I may be emotionally stunted, but I don't need any lessons from you about business,' he retorted. 'I've got an extremely successful company,' he said, pointing a finger at his chest, and then at her for emphasis. '*You've* got a piddling recruitment agency with no clients. Which of us do you think understands business better?'

He shook his head. 'I would moderate your ambitions, if I were you, Ms Thomas. You'll never get your agency off the ground if you're going to get all emotional and upset about every opportunity that comes your way.'

'I'll take my chance,' said Mary with a withering look. 'You're not the only employer in York, and if I'm going to be in business I'd rather deal with people who don't resort to blackmail as a negotiating technique!'

She turned to leave, wishing the floor didn't prevent her stalking off in her heels. 'Now, if you'll excuse me,' she said, 'I've wasted enough time tonight. My feet are killing me and I'm going home.'

* * *

'How's she been?' Mary tiptoed over to the cot and rested a protective hand on her baby daughter's small body, reassuring herself that she was still warm and breathing. She knew it was foolish, but she had to do it every time she went out, had to see Bea and touch her to reassure herself that she was all right.

She had asked her mother if she would ever get over the terror at the awesome responsibility of having this tiny, perfect, miraculous baby to look after, and her mother had laughed. 'Of course you will,' she had said. 'When you die.'

'She's been fine,' Virginia Travers said quietly from the doorway. 'Not a peep out of her.'

Reluctantly, Mary left her sleeping daughter and hobbled downstairs, collapsing on to the sofa at last with a gusty sigh. 'Thanks for looking after her, Mum,' she said as she rubbed her poor feet.

'It was no trouble,' Virginia said, as she always did, which always made Mary feel even guiltier. 'How did the reception go?'

Mary made a face. 'Not good,' she admitted. Disastrous might have been a more accurate reply, but she wanted to sound positive for her mother, who had enough to worry about at the moment.

Absently, she rubbed her arm where Tyler had grabbed her to stop her falling. It felt as if his fingers were imprinted on her flesh and it was almost a surprise to see that there were no marks there at all.

'It was a waste of time, really,' she told her mother.

'Oh, dear.' Virginia's face fell. 'It sounded such a good opportunity to make contacts too. There's no chance of a contract with Watts Holdings?'

Mary thought about Tyler's expression as she'd walked off. 'Er, no,' she said. 'I don't think that's at all likely.'

'Mary, what are you going to do?'

Her mother sounded really worried and Mary felt guilty about having blown her one chance to make an impression on Tyler Watts. At least, she had probably made an impression, but it wasn't the right one.

'Don't worry, Mum, something will come up,' she said, forcing herself to sound positive. 'There are still one or two companies I haven't approached yet, and I've placed a few temporary staff.'

All of whose contracts were up at the end of the next week.

Deciding to keep that little fact to herself, Mary found a smile of reassurance that she hoped would fool her mother, but when she looked closer she saw that Virginia was plucking nervously at the arm of the chair and avoiding her eye.

Mary straightened, suddenly alert. 'Mum?'

'Bill rang this evening,' Virginia told her a little tremulously. 'He wants to come home.'

'Oh, Mum…' Mary went over to sit on the arm

of the chair and put her arm around her mother's shoulders.

Virginia had been distraught when Bill had suddenly announced that he was leaving earlier that year. His decision had coincided with Mary's unexpected pregnancy, and coming back to York to have the baby had seemed the obvious solution.

Mary had needed somewhere to live and Virginia had needed the company, and in many ways it had worked as planned. Thirty-five was really too old to be living with your mother, and the house was too small for the three of them, but they had been rubbing along all right. Mary had even begun to think that her mother might be ready to move on. She had served Bill with divorce papers only the week before.

'What did you say?' she asked Virginia gently.

'I said I'd meet him tomorrow and we'd talk about it.'

Mary heard the wobble in her mother's voice and hugged her tight. 'You want him back, don't you?' she said, and Virginia's eyes filled with tears as she nodded.

'I know I ought to hate him after he hurt me like that, but I just miss him so much,' she confessed.

'Well, you need to talk about what happened, but you're still married,' Mary pointed out. 'If you decide you want him back and he wants to come

back, there's no reason you shouldn't just get on
with being married again.'

'He can't come back yet,' said Virginia, still a bit
tearfully. 'There isn't any room for him now.'

'Bea and I will move out. It's time we were doing
that anyway, and you certainly can't sort things out
with us around.'

'But you can't afford your own place,' her
mother objected.

'I'll work something out,' said Mary confidently,
giving her mother's shoulders a final squeeze and
getting to her feet. 'Don't worry about us, Mum.
You concentrate on sorting out things with Bill and
I'll find somewhere to live.'

But where? Mary asked herself wearily as she
started the long climb up the stairs to her office the
next morning.

She liked her attic office in the city centre.
Dating from the seventeenth century, the building
had higgledy-piggledy rooms, sloping floors and
dangerously low beams. It was charming but there
were times, like now, when she had Bea on her
hip and two bags to carry, that she wished for a
few more modern amenities. Like a lift, for
instance.

Plodding upwards, Mary made it to the first
landing and hoisted Bea higher on to her hip as she
pondered her accommodation problem. Her mother
was happy for the first time in months, and if she

and Bill had some space and some time on their own, Mary was sure that they could work things out.

If only Alan would release her money from the house, there wouldn't be a problem. As it was, Mary was beginning to wonder if she would ever get her money back. She had put the savings that she had into renting this office and getting the agency off the ground, but the only way that she had been able to afford that was living with her mother. She couldn't borrow while Alan was being so obstructive, and her income from the agency was sketchy, to say the least.

She had thought it was such a good idea to set up her own business when she moved back to York. It had seemed her best hope of generating an income while still giving her the flexibility to look after Bea herself, but perhaps she would have to think about applying for a job after all.

That wouldn't solve her immediate problems, though. It would take too long for her mother and Bill and, anyway, she would have to find a job that earned enough to cover childcare costs. What she needed right now was some money to put down as a deposit on a flat and cover the first few months rent until she had some proper income from the agency but, short of robbing a bank, Mary couldn't think where she was going to get it.

Her thoughts were still circling worriedly as she puffed up the last flight of steps and rounded the landing to stop dead when she saw who was waiting outside her office door.

'Oh,' she said. 'It's you.'

Her heart had lurched violently at the sight of him, leaving her breathless and a little shaken. Tyler Watts was the last person she had expected to see this morning.

He looked as grim as ever and his massive presence was overwhelming on the cramped landing. Mary was suddenly very conscious of the fact that her skirt was creased, her hair unwashed and she hadn't even had time to put on any lipstick.

She had overslept after a broken night and had fallen into yesterday's clothes as she hurried to get Bea ready for the day. Normally her mother would look after her, but Virginia was preoccupied with her coming meeting with Bill. Bea wasn't sleeping well at the moment and Mary would have been exhausted even if she hadn't had her own worries to keep her awake long after she had got the baby back to sleep.

She had spent half the night replaying that conversation with Tyler and wishing that she hadn't lost her temper. His attempt at blackmail had been outrageous, of course, but it wasn't as if he had been trying to force her into white slavery, was it? All he wanted was a bit of coaching.

Would a few tips on how to make a relationship work have been so hard to do? Mary asked herself.

It was only what she would discuss over a bottle of wine with her girlfriends, after all. They were all relationship experts now. And, in return, she could have had an introduction to Steven Halliday and a chance at a contract that would save her agency.

But no, she had had to get all righteous and uppity because he unnerved her. The way he was unnerving her now.

'What are you doing here?' she demanded rudely.

Tyler was looking from her to Bea. 'You've got a baby.'

'My, he's a quick one.' Bea got very heavy after three flights of stairs and Mary shifted her to her other hip. 'We can't fool him, can we, Bea?'

'Is she yours?'

'She is, and before you ask, no, her father's not around.'

Mary pulled her bag round and fished one-handedly for the key. Having already accused him of being a bully, a blackmailer and being emotionally stunted, it seemed a bit late to try sucking up to him, and she was too tired and fed up with her whole situation to make an effort any more.

'What do you want?'

'To see you,' he said and then looked at his watch. It was half past nine. 'Do you always start work this late?' he asked disapprovingly. In Tyler's world, everyone was at their desks at eight o'clock on the dot, and he was probably at his even earlier.

'No, not always,' said Mary, still searching for the key. 'It's been one of those mornings.'

Where was that key? She sucked in her breath with frustration. Of course, she hadn't had time to transfer the contents to a different bag so she was still carrying the one that had broken so inopportunely last night, and the muddle at the bottom was even worse than usual. She had managed to knot the broken strap together, but it hardly made for a professional image.

Still, it was too late for that.

This was hopeless, thought Mary, rummaging fruitlessly. She glanced at Tyler, still waiting for her to open the door. Her unwelcoming greeting didn't seem to have put him off, but then she guessed he was a man who didn't go until he had said what he was going to say.

'Look, would you mind holding her a moment?' she said, handing Bea over to him before he had a chance to answer. 'I'll just find my key.'

Appalled, Tyler found himself holding the baby, his arms extended stiffly so that she dangled from his hands. He stared at her nervously and the baby stared back with round eyes that were exactly the same grey as her mother's.

'Ah…here it is.' Mary produced the key from the depths of her bag and inserted it in the lock. She opened the door on to a room that was surprisingly light as the autumn sunshine poured through the two

windows set into the sloping roof, and she waved a
hand with a trace of sarcasm. 'Come into my luxury
penthouse,' she said.

CHAPTER THREE

TYLER was left literally holding the baby as Mary went in. He followed hastily and stood waiting for her to take it back, but instead she went over to the desk and switched on the computer.

'Er…Mary?' he said to remind her and she glanced up from her keyboard.

Good God, you'd think the man had never held a baby before! Mary smothered a smile. She had never seen anyone look so awkward with a small child. He was holding Bea at arm's length and his expression, normally so grim, was distinctly alarmed.

Who would have thought that a baby was all it took to put the ferocious Tyler Watts at a disadvantage? Pity she hadn't taken Bea with her last night. Things might have been very different.

As Mary watched, the alarm changed to horror as Bea's little face crumpled and, terrified that she was going to start crying, Tyler jiggled her up and down a bit. To his surprise, the baby paused, as if unsure how to react. For a breathless moment she looked extremely dubious and it was touch and go until, just as Tyler was convinced that she was going to bawl after all, she dissolved into a gummy smile.

Absurdly flattered, Tyler jiggled her up and down some more. Apparently deciding that this was a good game, Bea gurgled triumphantly. 'Ga!' she shouted, smiling, and, succumbing to that irresistible baby charm, Tyler smiled back.

Mary froze over her keyboard. She had never seen him smile before and the effect was startling, to say the least, lightening the grim lines of his face and making him look younger and more approachable.

And disturbingly attractive.

Swallowing, Mary straightened. She had wondered what he would look like if he smiled, and now she knew. Amazing what a mere crease of the cheek could do. Watching him smile was making her feel quite…unsettled. She wasn't sure it wasn't easier to deal with the grimly formidable Tyler than a Tyler who smiled like that.

'Coffee?' she asked in a bright voice and, reminded of her presence, Tyler stopped smiling abruptly. He flushed slightly, embarrassed at having been caught out playing with the baby.

'Thank you,' he said curtly, reverting to type.

Mary went over to fill up the kettle and tried not to feel put out that he would smile at Bea but not at her. She knew that he could do it now, so there was no excuse.

While the kettle boiled, she spread a rug on the floor and retrieved Bea from Tyler at last. The brush of their hands as he passed the baby back made her nerves leap alarmingly and she busied herself settling Bea on the rug and finding some toys for her to play with, and willing the heightened colour in her cheeks to fade.

'Sit down,' she said to Tyler, but without meeting his eye. 'I won't be a minute.'

Tyler nodded, but chose to walk around the room instead. It was very simply decorated in cream and the furniture she had chosen was simple and unfussy. Clearly a start-up operation, he thought.

He made himself think about the likely overheads of a business this size and not about the warm feeling Bea's smiles had given him, or the way Mary's top shifted over her curves as she stretched up to retrieve some coffee filters from the cupboard. Picking up a calendar from her desk, he pretended to study it, but he was very aware of Mary moving around, rinsing mugs, bending to find milk in the little fridge or chatting playfully to the baby, who was banging happily on the floor with a bright plastic ring.

The presence of the baby had thrown him, Tyler decided. He hadn't been expecting her or how warm and heavy she would feel between his hands. Mary

Thomas seemed to have a very odd idea about how to conduct business. He just needed a few minutes while she was making the coffee to collect himself and remember what he was doing here.

Mary studied him out of the corner of her eye as she waited for the coffee to drip through the filters. Tyler was probably used to freshly ground coffee, but that was too bad. He was lucky that he was getting coffee at all after last night!

What was he doing here anyway? She had been dismayed to see him, but what if there was a chance that she could somehow make up for the mistakes of last night? It seemed too good to be true, but why else would he be here?

She mustn't mess this up if she got another chance, Mary told herself sternly. With her mother so anxious to get back together with Bill, now was not the time to be taking high-minded stands on jobs. If she were to earn enough to get her and Bea somewhere to live, she would need to take anything she could get.

Tyler came back when the coffee was ready and took one of the easy chairs Mary used for interviewing. She would have preferred to sit behind her desk where she would feel more in control, but Bea might protest if she lost sight of her and, anyway, she reminded herself, she wouldn't give him the satisfaction of suspecting that he made her feel nervous.

So she sat opposite him and picked up her mug of coffee. 'What can I do for you?' she asked him.

Tyler was glad that he could get straight to the point. 'I want to offer you a deal,' he said.

'We discussed your idea of a deal last night,' Mary reminded him, cautious about getting her hopes up yet.

'I'm making a new offer.'

'Oh? Some new form of blackmail, perhaps?' she couldn't resist saying.

Tyler's eyes narrowed but he restrained his temper. Only the tic in his jaw indicated how difficult that was.

'No,' he said evenly. 'I'm prepared to offer you the recruitment contract for all junior staff in the York office if you will agree to give me some relationship coaching.'

Mary considered what he'd said. 'That's the same blackmail as before,' she pointed out.

'No, it isn't. Last night I said that I wouldn't give you the contract if you didn't agree. That was a threat. Now I'm saying that I'll give it to you if you do. That's an incentive. It's quite different.'

He paused. 'I'll also give you a lump sum—let's say ten thousand pounds—when I embark on a successful relationship, and if your advice leads to an engagement soon after that there'll be a further bonus.'

Mary stared at him, hardly able to believe what

she was hearing. Ten thousand pounds! Plus the income from that lucrative contract! Moving its headquarters back to York would make Watts Holdings one of the biggest employers in the city. The company was expanding dramatically and most of the new jobs would be at junior level. This would make her agency, she thought excitedly. She might not even have to rent. If she could get Tyler hooked up with someone nice, she could think about buying a small place for her and Bea.

And all she had to do in return was to teach Tyler a bit about how to keep a woman happy in a relationship. It wasn't what she had imagined herself doing, but it wasn't as if he was asking her to do anything immoral or unethical, was it? You could even say that there was something admirable about a man like Tyler putting so much effort into making a relationship a success.

'You must want this coaching very badly,' she said slowly, still hardly daring to believe that there wasn't a catch somewhere.

'I do.'

'But why do you want me? You could easily find someone with much better and more appropriate qualifications.'

Why *did* he want her? Tyler had been asking himself that all night. Because she was there, he had decided in the end. Because she seemed to know about coaching. Julia's words had been rankling and coming across Mary had seemed like the perfect opportunity to solve a nagging problem. Tyler wasn't a man who had reached the top by not grasping an opportunity when it came along.

Because he had decided that Mary was the coach he wanted, and he always got what he wanted.

Or it might have been because he hadn't been able to get her face out of his mind. He had kept hearing the scorn in her voice, remembering the directness of her grey gaze, and the way her eyes had danced when she had had the temerity to laugh at him.

'Because you're not afraid of me,' he told her in the end.

'I wouldn't be too sure about that,' muttered Mary.

'And I don't want to talk about feelings,' he went on, practically spitting out the word. 'I just want practical advice and you seem like someone who could give me that. Plus, you're available and have experience of coaching.'

'I don't have experience of the kind of coaching you mean,' Mary felt she should remind him. 'Not professional experience, anyway. I think most women my age get pretty expert at helping friends through relationship crises, but we tend to do it over a bottle of wine!'

She spoke lightly, but Tyler pounced on her comment. 'Exactly!' he said. 'And you're exactly the kind of woman I'm looking for. Well, not *you*, obviously,' he said quickly as Mary's brows shot up. 'But a woman like you. A bit younger, ideally, but professional and…you know, intelligent…*classy*,' he tried to explain.

Mary looked down at her crumpled skirt and top, which still showed traces of where Bea had gugged up some milk that morning, and boggled privately. She had never been called classy before.

'You said yourself that you talk to your friends about all that emotional stuff, and that means you'd know what women like that want from a man,' Tyler went on. 'At the same time, there's no risk of getting personally involved with you.'

'Why not?' asked Mary.

Tyler scowled, thrown by the directness of the question. 'Well, because you're not…you're not…' Damn it, she knew what he meant!

'Not attractive enough for you?' she suggested sweetly.

'Yes…I mean, no, you're very…' He hated being made to stumble and stutter and look a fool like this. 'Look, you're just not my type, OK? Just as I'm sure I'm not yours.'

'Quite,' said Mary, who was rather enjoying his discomfiture. It made up a little for being told that he found her completely unattractive. Not that she cared, of course, but still, a girl had her feelings.

'Besides, you've got a baby,' he said, indicating

Bea, who was thoughtfully sucking the leg of a stuffed elephant.

'Does that mean I can never have another relationship?' she asked innocently. 'I'm a single mother, yes, but I might be on the lookout for a father figure for Bea.'

She was only teasing, but a wary look sprang into Tyler's eyes. 'I'm not looking to take on another man's child,' he warned. 'I want my own family, not someone else's.'

'Well, that's us rejected, Bea.' Mary heaved a soulful sigh. 'It looks like it's going to be just the two of us.'

At the sound of her name, Bea took the elephant out of her mouth and beamed at her mother. Her smile was so sweet that Mary's throat tightened with such a powerful rush of love that she felt almost giddy. Reaching down, she smoothed the baby's hair with a tender smile.

When she glanced up once more, she saw Tyler watching them with a strange expression. 'It's OK,' she said patiently. 'I was just joking!'

'The condition of the deal is that our relationship is strictly a business one,' he said gruffly, more disconcerted than he wanted to admit by the sight of Mary leaning down to her baby. For a moment there, she had looked almost beautiful, her face soft and suffused with love and, when she'd looked up, the grey eyes had still been shining.

That luminous look was fading as she studied him, and he was vexed with himself for even noticing. What had he been expecting? That she would look that way at *him*?

'Fine,' she said. 'But what makes you think that I will agree this time?'

'I asked around last night,' he told her. 'Your business is in a bad way. You've got no long-term contracts.'

There was no point in lying about it. 'No,' Mary agreed, getting up to find some biscuits. She was starving, having skipped breakfast, and she couldn't concentrate properly without something to eat.

'I am prepared to consider your offer, but I need to know exactly what you want,' she went on, offering the packet to Tyler, who shook his head with a touch of disapproval.

Defiantly, Mary helped herself to two biscuits. They might be the last thing her figure needed, but a girl had to have *some* indulgences and, anyway, what difference was a pound or two going to make? She had already been told this morning that she was fat and unattractive and absolutely not Tyler's type. A biscuit here or there wasn't going to change that.

Not that she wanted it to change, of course.

'I've told you,' Tyler said with a trace of impatience. 'I want to get married.'

'But why?' she asked, brushing biscuit crumbs from her skirt. 'If you said you wanted to marry

X or Y, I could understand it, but you're just talking about "a wife" as if it doesn't really matter who she is. Why would you want a wife?'

'Because everyone else has one,' said Tyler. 'Because being successful now means having a wife and family, and I haven't got that.'

'There are other ways to be successful, though,' Mary pointed out. 'People who use their talents, people who are happy and contented with their lives…you can argue that they're the most successful people. You don't have to measure success against what others have.'

'I do,' said Tyler grimly. 'It was easy when it was just a question of having a bigger annual bonus or a faster car, but it's different now.'

'In what way?'

There was something disconcerting about the luminous grey eyes that were fixed on him and Tyler looked away, only to discover that the baby seemed to be watching him too. She had eyes exactly like her mother, he noticed.

Irritably, he got to his feet. He wanted to make Mary understand why it was so important to him to get married, and he couldn't do that with the baby distracting him.

'Last October I went to a reunion,' he said, marshalling his thoughts. 'We'd all done an MBA together a few years back.'

He hadn't wanted to go at first, but Mike had

talked him into it. 'Jack'll be there,' he had said. 'And Tony. They've both done incredibly well,' he'd added cunningly, knowing how competitive Tyler was. 'You'll be able to compare Porsches.'

So Tyler had gone along and it hadn't been too bad at first. Jack and Tony had indeed done well for themselves, but neither could rival the success of Watts Holdings.

'So your Porsche was bigger and better after all?' said Mary, following so far but not overly impressed. It was hard to care very much about the rivalry men felt over the size of their various toys.

'That's just it. No one was interested in talking about cars.' Tyler sounded so baffled that for a moment there Mary almost felt sorry for him.

'What were they talking about?'

'Babies.' He made it sound like aliens.

Mary couldn't help laughing. 'Really? I bet they were all still being competitive, though?'

'Oh, yes.' Tyler's mouth turned down. 'Who has the biggest/happiest/highest achieving family, who cried most when they saw their first child being born, whose child is most advanced—one was taking A levels in the womb, apparently.'

He stopped and looked down at Bea from his considerable height. 'I suppose yours is a super-achiever too?'

'No.' Mary smiled and retrieved the elephant that Bea had thrown at her feet. 'She's just a baby.'

She glanced back up at Tyler, who was looming over them both. 'It sounds as if it was a pretty boring evening,' she commented, 'but, other than that, what was the problem?'

What *had* been the problem? Tyler asked himself. It wasn't that he'd felt excluded. There was nothing new there. He was always the outsider.

And it wasn't that he'd been jealous. He had never wanted children.

But he didn't like not having what everyone else had. It had been easy before. Work until you could buy the biggest house, the best car, the fastest yacht. Now it was as if the rules had been changed when he wasn't looking. Success couldn't be measured by what you had bought any more. Suddenly it was all about families and children and relationships, areas in which he couldn't compete. He didn't even know the rules of the game.

Tyler didn't like that feeling.

But he sensed that if he was going to get what he wanted, he was going to have to be honest with Mary Thomas.

'The problem was realising that the game has changed. It's not about working hard and getting what you want any more. It's about being a different kind of person and I don't know how to do that,' he confessed in a burst of honesty.

'I thought it would be easy. If everyone was getting married and having a family, I could do that too.'

'It's never as easy as you think it's going to be,' said Mary, thinking of Alan.

'No,' Tyler agreed morosely.

The truth was that he couldn't bear the thought of being considered a failure. He knew that was how the other men had looked at him. His wealth, his spectacular success, had counted for nothing when compared with squatting in a birthing pool or changing a nappy.

Tyler had no intention of being a failure. If a family was what he needed to be considered a success, a family he would have.

He would have the best family ever. He would have the most beautiful wife, the most blessed of children. He would have it all.

That would show them.

But it wasn't proving as easy to acquire a wife as he had thought.

'I worked out a strategy,' he told Mary. 'First, I'd find someone to marry.'

'Good plan,' she said, her voice heavy with irony. 'It's always a good idea to choose a mother before you start the business of actually having children.'

Her sarcasm made Tyler shoot her a sharp look, but he decided to ignore it and get his story told so that could get out of here and back to work.

'I decided what kind of woman I was looking for,' he went on, determined to outline his careful strategy, but Mary interrupted him again.

'Let me guess!' she said, holding up her hand. 'You want someone young, beautiful, sexy, charming…what else? She probably needs to be intelligent—but not too clever, of course—feminine, but not too needy…am I close?'

Tyler eyed her with dislike. 'I wanted her to be good with children too.'

'Of course!' Mary snapped her fingers. 'How could I have forgotten? Naturally you'd need her to be a good mother as well as someone you can show off to all your colleagues.'

'Is that too much to ask?' he demanded, provoked.

'Have you met this paragon yet?' she countered.

'No,' he had to admit. 'That's the problem. I had plenty of girlfriends, but none of them were the kind of girls you'd want to marry, if you know what I mean.'

'No,' said Mary. 'What *do* you mean?'

'They were all young and pretty enough, but they were just out to have a good time, and that suited me. They were happy with being wined and dined and bought expensive presents. I want my wife to be classier than that,' Tyler explained haughtily. 'I want someone special.'

'We all want someone special,' said Mary.

Tyler ignored that. 'I started dating different women—attractive, professional women who had that kind of classiness and style. They're not hard to find.'

Mary could believe it. She had lots of wonderful, warm, intelligent, attractive friends who were finding it harder and harder to find a boyfriend.

And she was one of them, she realised with a shock. Well, not the attractive bit, according to Tyler, anyway. It was true that she was having trouble shifting the weight she'd put on when she was pregnant, and she was too tired most of the time to look stylish—witness her current outfit—but she had lots of friends who wouldn't hesitate to describe her as wonderful too.

She rubbed absently at the stain on her top, turning over the idea that she was once again a single woman. She had been with Alan for five years, and since then her world had been entirely occupied by Bea. There hadn't been time to think about whether she would ever find anyone else. Meeting a new man was right at the bottom of her priority list at the moment.

Which was just as well. Otherwise, it might have been mortifying to realise that she would never figure on Tyler Watts's wish list. Not that she would want to. Her own preference was for men with a little more warmth.

And then, for some reason, she found herself remembering how he had looked when he'd smiled at Bea, and a little *frisson* travelled down her spine.

OK, he had a nice smile. And a good body, she'd give him that. And, if she was being absolutely truthful with herself, there had been something about those big strong hands holding Bea that had given her a bit of a quiver too, but that was *it*, she reassured herself firmly. It wasn't enough to make him her type.

Not really.

Mary didn't like the way her thoughts were heading on this one, and distracted herself with another biscuit. 'With all this choice, why aren't you waltzing up the aisle right now?' she asked him indistinctly through the crumbs.

'I don't know, that's the problem.' Tyler sounded frustrated. 'It's always fine at first, but just when I begin to think that I might have found someone suitable, they start complicating things,' he complained.

'Complicating how?'

He hunched an irritable shoulder. 'They want me to *communicate* more, so that we can talk about our relationship, but it never seems to me that there's anything to say,' he said, sounding puzzled. 'I don't understand what the big deal is. We're sleeping together, we're going out to nice restaurants, we're having a nice time... What's the problem? But they get disappointed because I can't see the problem, and next thing there's a tearful scene and, before I know what's happening, they've gone and somehow it's all my fault!'

Tyler glowered. 'What am I doing wrong?' He started pacing again. 'This whole relationship thing is a mystery dreamt up by women, if you ask me,' he grumbled. 'Why does it always have to be so complicated?'

'Because people are complicated,' said Mary, handing Bea the elephant again.

'Well, I want the simple version,' said Tyler.

Mary sighed. 'The whole point about a relationship is that it's not just about what *you* want. You need to think about what your partner wants too— and maybe what she wants is for you to talk about how you both feel.'

'Right, that's the kind of thing I need to know.' Tyler swung round, relieved that they were getting somewhere at last. 'If I have to go through a whole lot of emotional mumbo-jumbo, I will. Everybody else seems to be able to do it, so there's no reason why I can't learn it too, is there?'

'You know, if you're going to think of my advice as mumbo-jumbo, I'm not sure we're going to get very far,' said Mary in a dry voice. 'It doesn't sound as if you're going to take it very seriously.'

'But I am,' he insisted. 'I'm deadly serious. I'll do whatever I have to do. You just have to tell me what women really want from a man, and I'll put it all into practice.'

'It sounds very easy when you put it like that,' she said.

'It will be easy,' he said confidently. 'I can't imagine an easier way to win a contract and ten thousand pounds, can you?'

Mary couldn't. 'No,' she admitted.

'So you'll do it?'

'On two conditions.'

Having got her agreement in principle, Tyler was prepared to negotiate. 'Which are?' he asked, sitting back down and then regretting it as Bea squawked with delight and promptly started crawling towards him.

'First, that we put a time limit on the exercise. I suggest two months,' said Mary coolly. She had been thinking while Tyler talked, and she hoped she could carry her plan off. 'A month for intensive coaching and a month for you to put it into practice, with my advice and feedback available if you're having problems.'

Tyler considered that. He didn't want to be spending months and months on this either. 'Fair enough,' he said, one eye on Bea, who had reached his shoes but had stopped there, to his relief. He had been afraid she'd want to get up on his lap.

'I'd want five thousand pounds at the end of the first month, regardless of whether you're in a relationship or not,' Mary went on, crossing her fingers. 'The other five thousand would be payable only if you were still in a relationship by the end of the second month.'

The pale blue eyes sharpened. 'My offer was ten thousand if I was settled in a relationship,' he reminded her.

'I know.' She met his eyes squarely. 'But that's my condition. Take it or leave it.'

Tyler studied her with new interest, unaware that Bea was pulling at his shoelaces. Take it or leave it was very much his own negotiating style, and very successful he had found it, but you needed to be in a strong position to carry it off. He wasn't sure that applied to Mary Thomas. Her business was clearly on a very shaky footing and she couldn't afford to risk losing the contract he was offering. He could beat her down easily.

On the other hand, he couldn't help admiring her guts. He liked people who were prepared to take a risk to get what they wanted. Mary was well aware that he had taken a risk in telling her as much as he had about himself, and he approved of her determination to make the most of her slim advantage. Besides, what was ten thousand to him?

'Agreed,' he said. He saw Mary's shoulders relax slightly as she let out a tiny breath of relief, and he very nearly forgot himself and smiled. 'What's the other condition?'

'That Bea and I move in with you for the first month.'

That did take him aback. 'Move *in*?'

'You've got a spare room, haven't you?'

'Yes,' he agreed cautiously, thinking of his ten bedrooms. 'But I don't see why we can't have our sessions in the office.'

'Because you can't treat it like learning a language or woodwork,' said Mary, who was wondering when he would notice that Bea had managed to undo both his shoes before crawling away to find her elephant again. 'Relationships are complex things. You can't divide them up into neat little segments, no matter how much some people, especially some men, would like to think that you can,' she added with a trace of bitterness. 'The only way for you to learn about relationships is for us to have one.'

Tyler immediately looked wary. 'I thought we'd agreed…?'

'Oh, not a physical one,' she interrupted him. 'I think we've established neither of us wants *that*.'

'Right,' he said, but not with quite as much relief as he would have expected.

He'd been honest when he said that she wasn't his type. He liked his women tall and blonde and elegant. Mary Thomas was none of those. She was on the short side of average and her curvaceous figure was…not fat, no, but definitely…*luscious* was the word that came to mind, and once it had lodged there it was impossible to shake it.

Her clothes were awful, true, and her hair needed a cut, but there was a softness and a warmth about her that contrasted intriguingly with the sharpness of her tongue and the quirkiness of her face.

So, while she might not be his type, there was something unnatural about the thought of going home to her every night and having to be relieved that he wasn't sleeping with her.

'I don't see why it's necessary,' he said, looking away from her.

Mary leant forward in her chair. Her mother needed this time alone with Bill to rescue her marriage and Mary was determined to make sure that she had it. That meant finding somewhere to go, and Tyler's house was the best option she had.

'Look,' she said, 'we've both got work to do during the day. Most relationships take place in the evening, and they're not just about sex. They're about learning to live together, to be aware of each other, to compromise. If I move in with you, you'll have to learn to do all those things and you can use me to practice your new skills.

'Of course it won't be an intimate relationship,' she went on persuasively, 'but it doesn't sound as if the physical side of things is your problem! What you need is practice communicating and listening and anticipating what the person you're living with really needs. Does that seem reasonable?'

'I suppose so,' said Tyler reluctantly.

'Living with me will mean that you have to do all of that, and if you *don't* do it it'll be my job to tell you. And, unlike in a real relationship, I won't get upset if you get it wrong because I won't have an emotional investment in you.'

It *could* work, Tyler admitted grudgingly to himself. There was even a bizarre kind of logic to it.

'What about the baby?' he said.

'She comes with me, of course.'

He eyed Bea dubiously. Having Mary in the house was one thing, but a baby…?

'I don't think my house is very suitable for a baby,' he said.

'What do you mean, *not suitable?*' demanded Mary. 'It's not as if she's a toddler who might break some of your ornaments. She's only just crawling!'

'It's not that.' Tyler didn't like being on the defensive, and he got restlessly to his feet, only to almost trip. *'What—?'*

Looking down, he saw that his shoelaces had been neatly untied and, with a muttered exclamation, he sat back down and did them up, knotting them with a savage yank.

Oblivious to his hostile glare, Bea batted her arms up and down with a crow of delight and would have set off towards him again if Mary hadn't intervened, scooping her up into her arms and trying not to laugh.

'She'll be a distraction,' Tyler said crossly, getting up once more and prowling over to one of the windows. It looked out over a cluster of rooftops to the Minster, its towers soaring proudly against a vivid blue autumn sky. He turned back to Mary. 'If I'm paying you all this money, I want you to concentrate on the job in hand.'

Unperturbed, Mary settled Bea on her lap and tried to distract her with her elephant. 'The job is to teach you how to have a relationship,' she reminded him crisply. 'And the first lesson you're going to have to learn is compromise.'

CHAPTER FOUR

'COMPROMISE?'

'Yes. You know what it means, don't you?'

Tyler scowled. 'Of course.'

Mary doubted if he had ever done it, though. Tyler Watts was not the compromising kind.

'Here's the deal, then,' she told him. 'I'm not going anywhere without my daughter, so you're going to have to decide whether you want me or not. Now, you may not want a baby around, but it's not just about what you want any more, is it? If our relationship is going to work, you've got to think about what I need and, in this case, I need to have Bea with me.'

'Why can't you be the one to compromise?' Tyler grumbled.

'Because my daughter isn't something I can compromise on,' said Mary. 'I can compromise on other things that don't matter to me so much, like how much time we spend together in the evenings, say, or when our deal starts.'

'It feels like it's started already!'

'Quite, which is why your first test is an important one.' She saw that he was looking mutinous, and sighed. Coaching a man like Tyler was going to be hard work. 'Look, imagine I'm your perfect woman,' she said, trying to make him understand. 'How much are you prepared to compromise to get me to live with you?'

'My perfect woman doesn't have a baby,' he pointed out, and Mary rolled her eyes.

'OK, what if she has a dog? Would you want a dog in your house?'

'No,' he said without hesitation.

'But what if this woman is perfect in every other way? She's gorgeous, talented, loving, clever…everything you've ever wanted, in fact. She adores you and makes you feel ten feet tall. Are you really going to give her up because she loves her dog?'

'If she adores me that much, she could give the dog up,' said Tyler facetiously, although he was secretly rather taken with the idea of someone adoring him.

'You can forget that,' said Mary. 'If she's a dog lover, there's no way she'll be giving up her dog for a man. No, it's down to you. What's the problem with a dog, anyway?'

'It'll make a mess.'

'So will children, and you say you want a family,' she pointed out. 'You're going to have to think very carefully about what really matters to you. I know what matters to me—my daughter—and that's where I'll refuse to compromise. What matters more to you than anything else? Your home? Your independence? Money?'

Tyler thought about it. 'Success,' he said at last.

'Right.' Mary suppressed another sigh. It was becoming clear why his previous relationships had never come to anything. 'If success means having this fabulous woman by your side, don't you think it's worth giving way on the dog thing if it means you get what you really want in the end?'

'I suppose so,' said Tyler grudgingly.

'That's compromise,' she said. 'It's all I'm asking you to do now. This is good practice for you, in fact.'

'Oh, all right,' he grumbled. 'Bring the baby— but keep her away from my shoelaces!'

Mary laughed. 'Honestly, you won't even know we're there most of the time.'

Tyler doubted that very much.

'Well, now that we've established that I do all the compromising and you get your own way,' he said a little grumpily, 'when do we start?'

Mary thought about it. 'Why don't we say Monday? That'll give me the weekend to get myself organised. Or is that too soon for you?'

He shook his head. 'The sooner we get started, the better, as far as I'm concerned.'

He was pleased that she didn't want to hang

around. Once he had a goal in mind, he liked to focus on it. The two month thing sounded good too, Tyler thought. He would pick up some tips the first month, and start a relationship the second. He did a quick calculation. If he applied himself, he could be engaged by Christmas.

Golden leaves swirled down like lazy confetti as the car spluttered up an avenue of lime trees and emerged at last in front of a beautiful Georgian mansion, its mellow red brick warm in the late afternoon sunshine.

Mary switched off the engine with a sigh of relief. Her car was on its last legs—or should that be wheels?—and the fifteen miles from York along winding country roads was about as much as it could cope with.

She just hoped it would be up to the journey every day. She couldn't think why Tyler didn't have an apartment in the city. It would be much more convenient, but then again, it wouldn't have the showy value of a house like this.

Mary had to admit that it was lovely. A flight of stone steps led up to a stately front entrance that in a more mundane house would be called a front door, and the tall windows were typical of Georgian grace and elegance. Mary had sometimes pressed her nose to exclusive estate agents' windows and seen houses like this, where no prices were ever mentioned. The implication was that if you had to ask, you couldn't afford it. It was the sort of house you visited on a Sunday afternoon, but not the kind of place you could imagine actually living in.

Unless you were Tyler Watts, of course. Mary wondered if he'd bought it because he thought it was beautiful, or because it was the biggest and best available.

'Ms Thomas?' A pleasant-looking woman had appeared at the door, and came down the steps to meet her as Mary lifted Bea out of the car. 'I'm Susan Palmer. I'm housekeeper here.'

Housekeeper, eh? Of course. Mary might have known Tyler would surround himself with flunkies to show how far he had come. He probably had a butler too, and an array of footmen and maids to tug their forelocks and say 'yes, sir, no sir' as required.

Freeing her hand, she offered it with a smile. 'I'm Mary,' she said, 'and this is Bea.'

'Welcome to Haysby Hall. Mr Watts said you would be coming.'

'He isn't here?' asked Mary, unaccountably put out.

'He doesn't usually get back until after I've gone,' Mrs Palmer explained. 'I leave a meal for him in the kitchen and he heats it up when he wants it.'

'Oh,' said Mary, digesting this. 'So you don't live here?'

'I live in the village. Mr Watts prefers being on his own. He values his privacy.'

So much for imagining Tyler surrounded by servants. It looked as if she'd been wrong about that.

It wouldn't be the first time, Mary reflected wryly, reaching into the car for the bag full of Bea's stuff.

Now she was going to have to think about the fact that she would be spending the next month out here alone with Tyler Watts. When she'd thought about it before, she'd just assumed that there would be other people around.

She would have to decide how she felt about that later.

'Is it OK if I use the kitchen when you're not here?' she asked Mrs Palmer as they walked towards the house. 'I need to prepare meals for the baby, and I like cooking for myself too.'

'Of course,' said Mrs Palmer. 'Mr Watts said you were to the treat the house as your own.'

She helped Mary carry all her things inside and showed her to a lovely bedroom with its own bathroom and smaller room next door for Bea.

'Is there anything else you need?' she asked Mary at last.

'No, I don't think so.' Mary was a little embarrassed at all the clutter she had brought with her. Most of it was Bea's and looked absurdly out of place in the gracious rooms. 'You've been very kind.'

'I'll be off then.'

Mary had secretly been longing for her to go so that she could explore properly. She and Bea spent a happy hour poking around the house, which was impeccably decorated. Clearly, a very expensive designer had been at work and no expense had been spared, but the final effect was rather like a show home for potential stately home owners. Mary couldn't find a single room that had an individual touch to it. It was quite a relief in the end to go back to her bedroom, even if the floor was covered with a cot, packs of nappies, feeding bottles, bibs and all the rest of the baby paraphernalia.

She had tidied most of it away, bathed Bea, fed her and put her to bed, and still there was no sign of Tyler. Beginning to feel distinctly peeved at his absence, Mary had a bath and changed into a loose skirt with a camisole worn under a dusky pink wrap-over ballet top.

She was just putting on some lipstick when she heard the crunch of tyres on gravel. It was dark by then, but the light pouring out of the downstairs windows was enough for her to see a silver Porsche park next to her battered old car. The next moment, Tyler got out and strode towards the door, disappearing out of Mary's sight.

There was the sound of the door closing and then silence. No call to find out where she was, or if she was all right. No honey-I'm-home. If Tyler was anxious to see that she had arrived safely, he was concealing it very well.

Mary's lips tightened. It was nearly half past eight and she had been here four hours. Stalking out on to the landing, she leaned over the elaborate balustrade. Tyler had found the letters waiting for him on the magnificent marble table in the hall and was leafing through them, apparently unaware of his duties as a host.

He must have heard her, because he glanced up. 'Oh, there you are,' he said, pushing the letters together and turning towards the room Mrs Palmer had pointed out as his study. 'I just need to make a couple of calls, then I'll be with you, OK?'

'No,' said Mary.

Tyler stopped, looking up over his shoulder with a distracted frown. 'No, what?'

'No, it's not OK,' she said and came down the stairs towards him

'What's not OK?' he asked, taken aback.

'Your behaviour,' said Mary succinctly.

'My *behaviour*?' he echoed incredulously. 'I've only been in the house a matter of seconds! How can I have done something wrong in that time?'

Mary surveyed him coolly. 'You weren't here to greet me when I arrived,' she told him, 'which means that I've been hanging around for nearly four hours, waiting for you to deign to come home. Now you want to come in and *ignore* me while you finish your business!

Tyler's face tightened with exasperation. 'You were the one who wanted to come out here,' he pointed out.

'And *you* agreed that the best way for you to learn about relationships was to pretend that we had one,' said Mary, reaching the bottom step. 'That relationship isn't going to last long if you think a few phone calls are more important than making me feel welcome. How do you think a real girlfriend would feel if you disappeared into the study as soon as you arrived without bothering to say hello?'

'I'm sure she would understand that I was probably busy,' said Tyler. 'As I *am*,' he added meaningfully but Mary refused to take the hint.

'I think it's more likely that she would think you rude and unfeeling,' she said. 'Why would she want to marry a man who would treat her like that?'

Tyler's jaw clenched with the effort of keeping his temper. 'Look, I'm only going to be five minutes,' he said. What could be more reasonable than that?

'That five minutes could be the kiss of death on your relationship,' said Mary and he scowled.

'Aren't you being a little overdramatic?'

'Tyler, do you want to learn how to have successful relationship with a woman or not?' she asked through gritted teeth.

'That's why you're here.'

'Quite, so I suggest that you listen to what I'm saying! What's the point of paying me to be your relationship coach if you're not going to take my advice?' she asked, exasperated. She put her hands on her hips. 'Let's start again. Imagine you're in love with me,' she ordered him. 'Go on!' she added as his jaw set in a stubborn line.

Tyler blew out an irritable breath, but turned obediently back to study her.

She looked different tonight, he realised, looking at her properly for the first time. Her hair was a soft cloud around her face, and she had abandoned that tight suit and was wearing instead a floaty sort of skirt and a top with a plunging neckline that emphasised her generous cleavage. Beneath it she wore a lacy camisole, the discreet glimpse of which hinted deliciously at hidden delights and made Tyler's head spin suddenly with images of sexy lingerie and silk stockings.

He swallowed. 'All right,' he said, 'I'm imagining.'

The odd thing was that the more he looked at her, the more he *could* imagine it. Not the whole being in love thing, obviously, but it wasn't that difficult to imagine wanting to kiss her, wanting to discover if those lips were as sweet as they looked, wanting to unwrap that top and see what that lace was concealing…

'I'm ready,' he said, annoyed to find that his voice was a lot huskier than it should have been.

'OK, now imagine how *I* feel,' she told him. 'We're deeply in love, remember. We can't keep our hands off each other and I haven't seen you since last night. I've spent all day looking forward to seeing you again. I've counted every minute.'

Getting into the part, she let a little wobble creep into her voice. 'I've come out to see your home for the first time, but you're not here to meet me when I arrive. I thought you loved me?'

Tyler was getting confused, not least by the way he couldn't rid his mind of the picture of not being able to keep his hands off her. It was disturbing to realise quite how vividly he could imagine it right now.

'I don't love you,' he said. He was on fairly sure ground there, surely?

Mary tsked. 'Not *me*, you idiot! We're pretending, remember?'

'Remind me why,' he said, weary of all the confusion.

'So that you can learn how to do it right when you come home to someone you really *do* love,' she told him. 'Now, I'm the love of your life and I'm feeling disappointed and unloved. What can you do to make me feel better? And here's a clue,' she added, not without a certain sarcasm. 'Disappearing into your study to make phone calls the moment you arrive is not the correct answer!'

Tyler rolled his eyes. 'All right, I need to pay you—her!—a bit more attention when I come home.'

'Exactly!' said Mary, pleased that he had got the point at last. 'I want to feel that you've been counting the hours too, that you're thrilled to find me here, that you can't wait to take me to bed...' She paused, listening to her words echoing uncomfortably around the hall. 'That is, *I* don't want that, of course,' she clarified carefully, 'but if I was in love with you, I probably would.'

'I see,' said Tyler dryly, not entirely sure that he did but unwilling to admit it, and distracted in any case by the idea of taking her to bed.

What would it be like to come home and find Mary waiting for him? he wondered. How would it feel if she were smiling, not criticising? If she opened her arms and let him kiss her? If he could run his hands over her warm curves, unwrap that top, slide off the silk and the lace and pull her upstairs to his room, so that they fell together on to his bed and he could lose himself in her softness and her warmth?

'Now, go outside and do it again.'

Tyler gulped and jerked back to attention. 'What? Do what?' he asked distractedly.

'Come in and greet me as if I'm the woman you want to marry,' said Mary patiently. 'Think of this as lesson one.'

'I thought compromising was lesson one?'

'OK, lesson two, then,' said Mary, rolling her eyes. 'This time, though, you've got a practical test. You've got to show your girlfriend—that's me— that you're thrilled to see her.'

'What am I supposed to say?'

'Make me believe that you love me,' she said. 'Starting with an apology is always a good move too.'

Still shaken by the vividness of his fantasy, Tyler let her push him outside, where he took some deep breaths of the cool autumn air. It smelt of damp leaves and woodsmoke, helping him pull himself together.

This was what he had wanted, he reminded himself. He had wanted practical advice on what to say and do in this kind of situation, and that was what Mary was giving him. He just hadn't counted on her being quite so distracting.

A few more breaths and Tyler had himself under control once more. This wasn't difficult. He should treat it as a challenge, and go in there and show Mary exactly what he could do.

Pushing open the door once more, he saw Mary at the foot of the stairs, looking so warm and inviting that all Tyler's fine speeches immediately went out of his head.

'Mary…' he said and stopped, realising that his lungs had forgotten how to work.

'Hi.' She smiled and came towards him. 'I was beginning to think you were never coming.'

Tyler managed to inflate his lungs. 'I'm sorry I'm late,' he said awkwardly. 'You look…gorgeous,' he said, and Mary paused for a moment.

'That's good,' she said. 'Very good, in fact.'

'No, I mean it.' Tyler stepped to meet her and took both her hands in his. 'I've been thinking about you all day,' he said. 'I was thinking about that suit you wear, and thinking about taking it off you, and now I come home and find you looking wonderful, and I still want to take it off you.'

'Yes, well, that's fine,' croaked Mary, trying, and failing, to tug her hands out of his, but Tyler ignored her.

'I've been thinking about touching you all day,' he said, his voice dropping until it seemed to reverberate in Mary's very core. 'I've been thinking about tonight and how it's going to be. Just you and me and a big bed.'

Mary gulped. 'Um, Tyler, I think that's probably—' she began, managing to pull her hands away at last, but he had released them only so that he could take her by the waist and pull her towards him.

'I've been thinking about this,' he said, bending his head and, although Mary opened her mouth, she had no idea either then or afterwards of what she was going to say. And, anyway, by then it was too late. Tyler's lips came down on hers and he kissed her.

Mary's heart seemed to stop with the shock and excitement that jolted through her at the first touch of his mouth. Her first thought was that Tyler was a great actor, her second that he was a great kisser and her third... Well, after the second she stopped thinking at all.

It was so long since she'd been kissed. She'd forgotten how good it felt to be held against a hard male body, to have strong hands sliding over you, round you, to pull you closer. His lips were cool and firm and very sure on hers. They teased and tasted and tested her resistance, which wasn't very strong, it had to be admitted.

There was something so seductive about being kissed like this. It was a game, a pretence, but shockingly intimate too, or that was how it felt to Mary. It didn't matter that Tyler Watts was practically a stranger, or that she didn't even like him that much. Right now, he was just a man and he was making her feel like a woman for the first time in a very long time.

Mary could have pulled back easily enough, but she didn't want to. She was tired of being sensible. Ever since Alan had thrown down his ultimatum she had held herself bottled in. She had focused on Bea and refused to let herself think about her own needs. Life was about being practical and getting through the day. It wasn't about yearning to be held or wanting to be touched.

But now she was being held and being touched,

and Tyler's kiss was like the first breach in a dam, where everything she had been keeping suppressed was building into a wave of sensation inside her, so powerful in its intensity that Mary would have been frightened if she had allowed herself to think about it. Instead, she gave herself up to the sheer pleasure of kissing and being kissed, of leaning into a strong, solid body and feeling her senses uncurl and shiver with delight.

And it was OK, because it didn't mean anything. It was just Tyler. It was just a pretence. They were playing a game, that was all.

Except perhaps they should have agreed on some rules before they started, like when they would stop, or how they would stop, and what they would say to make sure the other understood that it hadn't meant anything at all, that it was just a game…

In the end, it was Tyler who broke the kiss first. It took a huge effort of will for him to still his hands and loosen his hold on her warmth. Lifting his head slowly, reluctantly, he looked down into Mary's face.

Her eyes were dark, almost dreamy, her lips parted and he could see the heat flushing pink beneath her skin. It was all he could do not to kiss her again.

He felt ridiculously shaken. He hadn't really been thinking. He had walked in all ready to pretend, and in the end it had been easy enough to imagine how he would react if he had been waiting for her all day, how good it would be to see her, to be able to touch her and then... Well, dammit, he was only doing what she had told him, wasn't he?

Imagine you're in love with me, she had said. So he had.

He just hadn't expected how warm and soft and *sexy* she would be, how sweet she would taste, how she would melt like fire in his arms. He hadn't expected it to feel so good, so alarmingly *right*, to kiss her, and now all he could do was look down into her face, unable to think of a single thing to say, other than to wish that he could kiss her again.

Mary found her voice first.

'Very good,' she said. Her voice was a bit squeaky but, under the circumstances, she didn't think it sounded too bad. She cleared her throat. 'That was really quite convincing.'

Tyler felt a stab of something—relief that she had just been pretending too, he told himself.

At least he hoped it was relief. It had felt perilously close to disappointment and he didn't want that.

Belatedly realising that he was still holding her, he let Mary go and stepped back. 'I'm glad you approve,' he said.

'I certainly do.' Mary was relieved to hear herself sounding positively composed, which was quite something when her blood was still thrumming and her heart thumping and every nerve in her body was screaming at her to leap into his arms and cling on to him until he promised to kiss her again and not stop, ever.

'Go to the top of the class,' she said.

Tyler Watts might be useless at emotions, but he clearly wasn't useless when it came to the physical side of a relationship. Somehow she hadn't thought anyone so brusque would be such a good kisser. She would have expected him to be rough and as careless of feelings as he was at work, but he hadn't been like that at all. He had been slow and sure and sensuous. If he kissed like that, what would it be like when he made love?

Mary swallowed as an image of Tyler making love to her presented itself with uncomfortable clarity. He must be really, *really* bad at the emotional stuff, she thought, for all those ex-girlfriends to walk away.

'Can I go and make those phone calls now?' he asked.

A bucket of cold water dashed in her face could hardly have been a more effective return to reality. Tyler was back to business.

Mary thought she had done pretty well just to stay upright, and at least she had managed to keep *some* grip on the fact that the kiss had just been part of the pretence, but Tyler made her efforts look absolutely pathetic! He had probably been thinking about his phone calls all along.

Good, Mary told herself. That made it easier for her to stay cool and professional, the way they had agreed.

And the sooner he went, the sooner she could sit down. Her legs were trembling so much she was afraid that she would crumple to the floor any minute, and how cool and professional would that look?

'I think you've done enough of the devoted lover bit for now,' she agreed. 'Mrs Palmer left a meal which just needs heating up,' she added as he turned towards his study once more. He wasn't the only one who could do practicality. 'When do you usually eat?'

'When I'm ready.' Tyler looked at his watch. 'There are a few things I want to catch up on. Let's eat about half past nine.'

Something in the quality of Mary's silence made him look at her. 'What?'

'A better reply would have been, Are you hungry?' she said. 'Or, When would *you* like to eat? Just a suggestion,' she added sweetly. 'Something for you to bear in mind when you have someone you want to impress here.'

'Oh. Yes.' Tyler grimaced at having been caught out again. Clearing his throat, he tried again. 'When would you like to eat, Mary?'

'About nine would be nice,' she replied, equally polite. 'I'll see you in the kitchen then, shall I?'

In fact, it was just before nine when Tyler made his way to the kitchen. It wasn't that he didn't have lots to do, but he hadn't been able to concentrate with Mary in the house. She wasn't making a noise, but just knowing that she was there was a distraction.

He'd been trying to read a report at his desk, but it was hopeless. The words kept shimmering in front of his eyes and he'd end up thinking about that tantalising glimpse of lace, about how soft she had been beneath his hands, about how good it had felt to kiss her.

This was ridiculous, Tyler reminded himself irritably. Mary Thomas was not part of his strategy, or only in an advisory role. She wasn't his kind of woman. He was looking for someone gracious and elegant, not a chaotic single mother, no matter how good she might feel.

It had probably been a mistake to kiss her, but he had only been proving a point, he managed to convince himself at last. It clearly hadn't meant anything to Mary, anyway. She had been cool as a cucumber afterwards. Tyler glowered down at the page he'd been trying to read for the last twenty minutes. There was no reason for either of them not to be cool. They had both been pretending.

Hadn't they?

Of course they had.

Tyler closed the report and slapped it down on to the table with an irritable exclamation. It was hopeless trying to read this now. He would go and have something to eat, remind himself of all the reasons he wasn't interested in Mary Thomas, and then come back and work.

He found Mary in the kitchen and paused in the doorway, astounded at the transformation in the room. He only ever came into the kitchen to use the fridge or the microwave, and it had never struck him as a room he would spend any time in. But Mary had pulled the blinds and switched on the concealed lights under the cupboards so that the kitchen looked positively cosy. The table was laid for two, with glasses and a candle, and an appetising smell wafted from the oven.

And then there was Mary herself. Wrapped in Mrs Palmer's striped apron, she was measuring vinegar into a little bowl and humming happily to herself and her presence seemed to suffuse the room with a warmth it had never had before.

Tyler cleared his throat and she jerked round, breaking off in mid-hum. 'Oh…hi,' she said after the tiniest of pauses. It took a huge effort to keep her voice neutral when every nerve she possessed had sprung to attention at the sight of him and her heart was blundering around in her chest, bouncing off her ribcage and generally behaving like a hyperactive puppy.

She turned back to the dressing she was making. 'You don't mind eating in the kitchen, do you?' she asked, super-casual. 'I thought it would be cosier than the dining room.'

'Here's fine,' said Tyler, coming into the kitchen. 'I usually take a plate back to my study and eat while I work.'

'Really?' Mary glanced at him in surprise. 'I imagined you dining in solitary splendour in that wonderful dining room, having a five-course meal served by a butler!'

'No.' He hunched a shoulder in what Mary was coming to recognise as a characteristic gesture. 'I'm not comfortable with servants. I prefer to have the house to myself.'

'Mrs Palmer said you valued your privacy.' She hesitated. 'Is that why you didn't want us here?'

'Partly,' said Tyler, although he wasn't sure that was strictly true. He couldn't admit that he'd been afraid that she would change things just by being here, and of course that was exactly what she had done. She'd only been here a matter of hours and already the house felt subtly different.

'But you're not here as a servant,' he went on. 'I don't like being waited on. It makes me realise I don't know the right knife and fork to use, or which way I should be passing the port.'

It was a surprising glimpse of vulnerability from such a hard man, thought Mary. She wouldn't have expected him to give a toss about what other people thought of him.

'Don't you have to do a lot of entertaining?'

Tyler's mouth turned down at the thought. 'I get

a cook in and extra staff to serve if that happens, but I try to avoid all that as much as I can.'

'It's a shame,' said Mary lightly. 'It's a perfect house for parties.'

'I can't stand all that socialising and chit-chat,' he grumbled. 'I never know what to say.'

'You didn't seem to have any trouble talking to me the other night,' said Mary, grinding salt and pepper into her dressing.

'That was different,' said Tyler, although he wasn't sure how. He just knew that it had been.

'Perhaps you should try blackmailing all your party guests,' she suggested mischievously. 'That seemed to be a good way to keep the conversation going!'

'It seemed to work with you anyway,' Tyler agreed, and to Mary's dismay he smiled, the same startlingly unexpected smile as before. She wished he wouldn't do that, just when she'd got her breathing under control again.

She busied herself searching in the cupboards for mustard and honey and willed her heartbeat to slow.

'It's a big house for one person. Don't you ever get lonely here?'

Tyler shrugged. 'I'm used to being on my own.'

Mary located some mustard and straightened. 'Well, I'll try not to disturb you too much while I'm here.'

She could try, but Tyler doubted very much if

she would succeed. She'd only just arrived and she was already disturbing him far more than he wanted to admit.

CHAPTER FIVE

'You'd better get used to having other people in the house,' Mary went on, determinedly cheerful.

'Why's that?' asked Tyler warily.

'If you're going to have a wife and children, you'll soon fill up all those rooms,' she told him. 'You'll have to wave goodbye to your peaceful life then!'

He didn't look as if he found the prospect very appealing.

'I suppose so,' he said, with a marked lack of enthusiasm.

He tried to imagine being married. There would be another woman in the kitchen then, but when he tried to picture her, all he could see was Mary, with her cloudy hair and soft curves and dancing grey eyes.

Searching around for a change of subject, he spotted the glasses on the table. 'Would you like me to find a bottle of wine?'

'That would be lovely,' Mary answered.

'I'll just go and find one.'

He was back a few minutes later, blowing dust off

a bottle with an eye-popping label. Of course, she should have known that he would have a fully stocked wine cellar, because that was what you had when you'd made it. He probably had a string of racehorses too, although Mary was prepared to bet he never took time off to go the races.

'I was thinking more of a bottle of plonk,' she said when he showed her the bottle.

'I haven't got anything cheap,' he said haughtily. 'We may as well have this.'

Mary put the salad on the table and watched him out of the corner of her eye as he found a corkscrew and opened the bottle. He moved with a lightness surprising in one of his rocklike build, and there was an economy and a control to his movements that Mary could only envy.

He was a complicated man, she thought. Complex and difficult; it was easy to be overwhelmed by his forbidding personality and miss the vulnerability underneath. Who would have thought that he would be a man who ate his meal alone at his desk, for instance, or who cared if people noticed that he was using the wrong knife?

Who would have thought that he would be such a good kisser?

She wasn't supposed to be thinking about that kiss, Mary reminded herself sternly and busied herself putting the salad together and taking Mrs Palmer's lasagne from the oven.

But the more she tried not to think about it, the more her eyes kept snagging on his hands, deft as they spun the bottle, twisted in the corkscrew and eased out the cork with a deliciously soft pop. She couldn't help remembering how warm they had felt through her top, how insistent against her spine, how sure cupping her breast.

Wrenching her eyes away, Mary set the lasagne on the table, where it made an absurd contrast with the expensive wine that Tyler was pouring into the two glasses.

'Try it,' he said, and she paused to take a sip. It was like no wine she had ever tasted before, velvety soft and smooth and utterly delicious.

It was nearly as good as kissing him.

Stop it, Mary scolded herself furiously. Stop it at once. He's your client, that's *all*.

Taking another sip of wine to steady herself, she sought around for a subject of conversation that would take her mind off Tyler, sitting solid and formidable on the other side of the table.

'Do you mind if I do some cooking while I'm here?' she asked at last, helping herself to lasagne and trying to keep her eyes off his hands.

'No,' said Tyler. 'But there's no need if you don't want to. Mrs Palmer is a perfectly adequate cook.'

'I know, but I love cooking and it would be a real treat to use a kitchen like this. Mum's only got a tiny galley.' She looked around her enviously. 'This is a wonderful kitchen. It's an amazing house, in fact. It'll be a great place to bring up a family. There's so much space here, and the house is just crying out to be full of people and noise and laughter. You're very lucky,' she told him.

'I'm not lucky,' said Tyler flatly. 'I've just worked hard to get what I want.'

'Maybe the luck is in having the personality to stay focused on what you want,' Mary suggested. 'Half the time I don't even know what I want. I'm too busy just getting from day to day.'

'You must have some kind of goal.'

'I suppose I do, but it's not a very grand or ambitious one,' she said. 'I'm not like you. I don't have to be the best.' She sipped at the wine reflectively. 'I just want a little house I can call my own where I can bring Bea up and…well, just be happy.'

'Aren't you happy at the moment?'

Mary sighed a little as she picked up her fork and tucked into the lasagne. 'I think I've been too worried about money recently to be really happy,' she said, aware that the wine had loosened her tongue, but too tired of keeping it all to herself to care.

'I've been living with my mother since I came back to York,' she told Tyler. 'She's been fantastically supportive, and I don't know what I would have done without her, but the house isn't that big, especially with all the clutter you accumulate with a baby. We do get on top of each other a bit.'

Putting down her fork, she took another sip of the wine, which was slipping down very nicely indeed. She was feeling better already.

'I'm desperate to find my own place but I haven't been able to afford to buy, or even rent. Until now, that is,' she said, smiling at him. 'I'm hoping that will all change now that I've got the contract with Watts Holdings. I'll start to get some income from the agency—and of course my coaching fee will help too!'

Her smile had an odd effect on Tyler, and he tried to hide it with a reproving look. 'An agency is a risky thing to start up if you don't have any capital.'

'I realise that now,' she said ruefully. 'But it seemed like a good idea at the time. I thought that it would be a good way to use my personnel experience but still keep my independence.

'Childcare is so expensive nowadays,' she said with a sigh. 'It wouldn't be fair of me to rely on Mum, and I'd have been lucky to have got the kind of salary that would have enabled me to pay someone to look after Bea while I was at work. And if I *had* got a well-paid job, I'd have had to work so hard I wouldn't have enough time with Bea. I didn't want that. I thought the agency would give me some flexibility. I could take Bea with me sometimes, or work from home if I had to.'

Her glass was empty and Tyler reached over with the bottle to top it up. 'I don't understand why you're having to do everything on your own,' he said. 'Where does Bea's father figure in all of this?'

'He doesn't,' said Mary, and her face closed.

Tyler cursed himself. What was it Julia had said? The social skills of a rhinoceros. At times like this he wondered if she was right.

'Sorry,' he apologised gruffly. 'It's not my business. I shouldn't have asked.'

'It's OK.' Mary's expression relaxed slightly. 'You're showing an interest and asking me about myself and, as your relationship coach, I approve of that! And I don't mind talking about Alan, not really. For a long time I couldn't talk about anything *but* Alan.'

'Alan being Bea's father?'

She nodded. 'I met him in London. He's a psychologist by training. My company sent me on a coaching course that he was running, and I thought he was brilliant.'

Her face softened, remembering how dazzled she had been. 'Alan's one of the cleverest people I've ever met. And he's got a kind of charisma… It's difficult to explain,' she said. 'He really understands people and what makes them tick, and he's got a fantastic ability to help people think clearly about what they want and how to realise their dreams. You'd get on well with him.'

Tyler didn't think so. The man sounded a complete wimp to him.

'I was incredibly flattered when Alan suggested I train as a coach myself and go and work with him,' Mary went on, unaware of Tyler's mental interjection. 'He wanted to expand his company to offer a wider range of courses, and I could be part of that. It was a really exciting time for me.'

'But it wasn't just a professional relationship?'

'No.' Mary gave a self-deprecating grimace. 'I know it's hard to believe now!'

Tyler frowned. 'Why?'

'Well, you know…' She gestured at her hair and then down at her clothes. 'I'm such a mess. Mum says I've let myself go since having a baby, and I suppose it's true.'

He had thought she looked a mess at the reception, Tyler remembered. And when he had been to see her at her office she hadn't looked any better groomed. It was true that her hair could do with a good cut, and she didn't have the kind of style he usually admired in a woman, but she looked different tonight. He couldn't put his finger on why.

It was that damned bit of lace, Tyler decided. He was too distracted by it to think analytically.

'You don't look a mess now,' he said abruptly. 'You look…' *Warm. Sexy. Alluring.* '…fine,' he chose in the end.

Mary paused with the glass at her lips and looked at him over the rim. Her eyes were wide and a lovely shimmering grey, and Tyler found his gaze caught in them for a long jangling moment.

'Thank you,' she said, putting the glass down a little unsteadily. 'That was kind of you, but you really don't need to be polite. It's only me!' She felt ridiculously shaken by that meeting of their eyes, and that was stupid because he was, after all, a man who could kiss her until her bones melted and then calmly walk off and make phone calls.

The only way to deal with it was to make a joke of it, she decided. 'For future reference, though, no woman ever wants to hear that she looks "fine",' she told him in her best teacher mode. 'When your fiancée asks you how she looks, try and think of a different adjective—and not "nice"!'

'What should I say?' asked Tyler. 'Beautiful? Gorgeous?' His eyes dropped to the lacy camisole. 'Sexy?'

His voice seemed to reverberate down Mary's spine in the fizzing little silence that followed. This is a lesson, she told herself with an edge of desperation. It's not real. He doesn't really think you look gorgeous or sexy. How could he?

Inhaling slowly, she pinned on a smile. 'Any of those would do perfectly. Where were we?' she added brightly.

'You and Alan were having a relationship,' he reminded her in a dry voice.

'Oh, yes. Well, I was madly in love with him, of course.'

Tyler stabbed a piece of lettuce. 'Why "of course"?'

'Because Alan's like every woman's dream,' she said simply. 'He's good-looking and witty and clever—he's one of the most intelligent people I know. He runs a very successful business, he knows about food and wine, he's well-travelled and cultured…'

Mary's smile was twisted with sadness as she remembered how dazzled she had been. 'But the best thing about Alan is that you can *talk* to him,' she said. 'He really listens to what you say. You've no idea how rare that is in a man,' she added wryly.

He was listening to her, Tyler wanted to say, but Mary was still going on about the perfect Alan.

'I couldn't believe that someone like Alan would be interested in me,' she said. 'When he told me that he loved me and asked me to move in with him, I was over the moon, and it seemed like the obvious solution for both of us. He was struggling to pay his mortgage after the divorce, so it was easier for me to contribute to the running costs and put a bit towards the mortgage myself.'

She could see Tyler looking disapproving already at the idea of such a casual financial arrangement.

'It meant that I could live in a nice house, but it was about more than that,' she tried to explain. 'Paying towards the mortgage felt as if I had a real stake in his life, and that we were committed to each other, even though it was too soon after his divorce to think about getting married. All I wanted was to be with him.'

'So what put an end to this idyll?' asked Tyler grouchily.

'I got pregnant.' Mary turned her glass between her fingers, her eyes on the ruby liquid. 'It was an accident. Alan had made it clear right from the beginning of our relationship that he didn't want children.'

'Why not?'

'He's a bit older than me and he's got three children in their late teens from his marriage. He said he thought three was enough, and that he was too old to deal with all the broken nights and toddler tantrums again. And I was fine with that,' said Mary. 'Having children had never been something I'd dreamed of, and I was so in love with him then that I didn't care about anything as long as I could be with him.'

Tyler made a sound somewhere between a snort and a grunt. He was getting a bit sick of hearing about how much Mary loved Alan.

'So what happened?'

'I was thirty-four. It wasn't exactly my last chance to have a baby, but I had a real sense that it was now or never, and I realised then that I didn't want it to be never.'

She lifted her shoulders slightly, apparently

unaware of how the movement deepened her cleavage and revealed a bit more of the lacy camisole. Tyler made himself look away.

'Alan didn't see it my way,' she said. 'He said that he had always made it clear that he didn't want any more children, and that was true, he had. He told me that I would have to choose.' Mary swallowed, remembering the painful scene. 'It was him or the baby. I couldn't have both.'

'And you chose the baby?'

'Yes,' she said, letting out a long breath. 'I chose Bea. And I've never regretted it, not for a second.'

'Even though she cost you the love of your life?'

Mary looked sad. 'Yes, even though it meant I lost Alan. I'd hoped that once the baby was born he'd change his mind, but he's refused to even acknowledge her.'

'He's still obliged to support her,' Tyler pointed out, but she shook her head.

'I don't want any support from him. It was my choice to have the baby, and I'll support her by myself. I wouldn't take maintenance from Alan, even if he were to offer it, which he won't. He said he didn't want anything to do with her.' Her voice quavered at the memory.

Tyler was unimpressed. 'If he felt that strongly about having children, he could have had a vasectomy,' he pointed out. 'Bea's his daughter whether he likes it or not, and he ought to provide you with some financial support at the very least.'

'I don't want it.' Mary's mouth set in a stubborn line. 'Alan said I wouldn't be able to manage on my own with a baby, and I'm going to prove him wrong.'

'Maybe,' Tyler allowed, 'but it sounds as if you're struggling.'

'Only because Alan's quibbling about the money I put into the house and the company.'

She couldn't believe that she was telling him all this. It must be the wine, Mary decided. It was so mellow and delicious that she had got to the bottom of another glass without even noticing. She had better not have any more.

'I didn't just lose Alan,' she told him. 'I lost my job and my home and my savings, although I'm hoping I'll get some of those back eventually.'

Tyler was appalled. 'You lost your *job*? Even I don't sack staff when they get pregnant!'

'I wasn't exactly sacked,' said Mary, amused in spite of herself. The 'even I' spoke volumes! 'But it would have been too difficult carrying on working with Alan under the circumstances. It's one of the disadvantages of sleeping with the boss,' she added with a dry look.

'What's happened about your money?'

'Nothing as yet. Alan agreed to buy me out of the house—it was his home before I came along and he needed somewhere his children could go and stay, so that seemed fair—so I moved in with a friend, but it was clear that I couldn't stay there for ever and I wasn't sure how I was going to cope after the baby was born. I didn't have any income so I would have to go back to work as soon as I could.

'It was about then that my stepfather left my mother. She was distraught, and it seemed to make sense for me to come back to York and be with her. I'd be company for her, she could help me look after the baby, and if nothing else it would be cheaper than London, but I think it may have been a mistake. Once I had somewhere to go, Alan stopped feeling guilty and it allowed him to drag his feet about buying out my share of the house.'

Tyler was looking very disapproving by now. 'You should have a legal claim on the house. Didn't you have a proper contract drawn up?'

'I should have done, but I didn't,' said Mary. 'It was stupid of me, but we were so happy together that it never occurred to me that I would need it. Alan says he will repay my share, but first he has to have the house valued, and he's quibbling about how much money I actually put in…'

She sighed. 'I know he's angry but I never thought that he would be so petty and so mean. It's not as if we're talking about a huge amount of money but it would have helped me get a place of my own here. As it is, I'm reduced to forcing myself on you for a month,' she said with a wry smile.

'I'm hoping my mother and stepfather will be able to sort out their problems, but they need to be able to do that without Bea and me sharing the same very small space. Moving in here seemed like my best option, but I didn't take into account the fact that you'd prefer to be on your own. I'm sorry,' she finished apologetically.

'It's not going to be a problem,' said Tyler gruffly. 'In fact, I think you're right about it being the best way to coach me. I feel as if I've learnt a lot about relationships already tonight.'

'Good.' Mary smiled, glad to be able to lighten the atmosphere and shift the conversation away from the sorry mess she'd made of things lately. 'Well, that's what I'm here for! You're going to be so clued up on relationships by the time I leave, the next woman you date will be a very, very happy woman!'

And if Tyler made love the way he kissed, she would be a very lucky woman too.

Mary swallowed the last of her wine in a gulp and pushed that thought aside. She was lucky too, she reminded herself sternly. She had Bea, and by the end of the month she would have five thousand pounds to put down on a flat of her own. What more could she want?

Mary's mind flickered towards Tyler and she was revisited by a sharp, shivery memory of that kiss before she wrenched it determinedly away. She wasn't even going to *go* there. A healthy baby and somewhere to live. She would be perfectly content with that.

Mary lifted her baby daughter out of the bath and wrapped her in a warm towel. She loved this part of the day. Bea was always sweet-smelling and smiley, squealing with delight at the games Mary played with her.

It had been a busy day, but a productive one, and Mary felt pleasantly weary. It felt good to know that things were happening at last.

Tyler had been long gone by the time she and Bea had made it down to the kitchen to find some breakfast. They'd found Mrs Palmer there, very concerned that Mary had cleared up the night before.

'You should have left everything,' she protested.

'It was only a matter of stacking the dishwasher,' said Mary. 'Honestly, it was no trouble. I wouldn't have felt comfortable leaving the kitchen in a mess.'

Anyway, there hadn't been anything else to do. Tyler had disappeared back to his study and Mary had been left wishing that she hadn't drunk the wine so quickly, or told him quite so much about her muddled affairs.

She had sat in a beautifully decorated sitting room for a while, but she'd been unable to settle. Normally time to read a book was an unimaginable luxury and it had been frustrating to find the type dancing before her eyes. She'd kept imagining what it would be like if Tyler was sitting there with her.

Perhaps she should have suggested that? After all, if it were a real relationship he wouldn't spend his evenings working. They would be curled up together on the sofa in front of a fire. She would be able to slip her arm over that broad chest and feel the hard, masculine solidity of him, and then her face would be at just the right angle to press into his throat and smell his skin.

She could kiss that pulse below his ear and then feather her lips along his jaw to his mouth, teasing and tantalising until she felt his mouth curve in a smile beneath hers, and then *he* could tip her abruptly beneath him, pulling her down into the softness of the big sofa and running his hands up from her ankle, tracing delicious patterns behind her knee, sliding beneath her skirt and drifting upwards in insistent exploration, and she would unbutton his shirt with unsteady hands and all the time they would be kissing, kissing the way they had kissed in the hall, but this time there would be no reason to stop and he would—

Mary had shut her book with a snap. This had to stop, and right now.

Think Mary, she'd told herself. This is a man who is looking for a leggy, slender, well-groomed blonde with no children and a hard-headed attitude to marriage, a man who has told you quite frankly that he doesn't find you attractive. He's a ruthless, arrogant workaholic with all the charm and sensitivity of a bulldozer.

A man who kissed you until you were weak at the knees and then went off to talk business on the phone.

On a scale of one to ten, she'd asked herself, how sensible is it to start fantasising about him making love to you on a sofa?

Minus three hundred and forty-two, at least.

You're here to do a job, Mary had reminded herself sternly. And that's *all*.

Which was all very well, but a pain when you had to spend your entire time remembering to remember. Too often during the day, Mary had been aware of a small fizzy feeling deep inside at the thought of seeing Tyler again that evening. Whenever she caught her mind drifting that way, she would sit up with a start and make herself get back to work, but it was exhausting having to be constantly vigilant with her own thoughts.

Still, when she hadn't been wasting time trying not to think about Tyler, it had been a good day. Most of it had been spent in a flurry of activity, contacting prospective staff and arranging interviews. Bea had been obliging. She had either slept or been happy to play with her toys, and at lunchtime Mary had pushed her to the Museum Gardens to enjoy the autumn sunshine while it lasted.

'I don't know what I'm going to do with you tomorrow, though,' Mary told her as she dried her little toes. She had a meeting with Steven Halliday at Watts Holdings to talk about the new contract and assess their requirements, and it would be hard to strike the right professional note if she had Bea with her. Her mother was the obvious fallback position, and Mary didn't really think that she'd mind, but when she'd rung there had been no reply. 'Your granny isn't answering the phone.'

Bea squealed and batted her arms in reply. She loved being part of a conversation.

'Do you think she's out gadding around with Bill?'

'Ga!'

'I've asked her to ring me back, but if she doesn't get home until late I'm just going to have to take you with me, and it would be very, very good if you felt like having a sleep then.'

'Ga, ga, *wa*!'

Kneeling beside her, Mary smiled down at her daughter, who was kicking her legs on the towel. Lucky Bea, who didn't have to worry about childcare or contracts.

Or how to achieve just the right balance between friendliness, professionalism and nonchalance when Tyler came home.

Mary glanced at her watch. If yesterday was anything to go by, she had nearly three hours to calm the pathetic butterflies in her stomach. He wouldn't kiss her again. They had done greetings yesterday.

And that was a good thing, of course.

'A very good thing,' she said out loud to Bea, tickling her feet and making her crow with laughter.

'What do we care, anyway?' she asked her, as Bea squirmed with pleasure. 'We're going to find a lovely flat just for us, and we'll have fun there, won't we?'

Talking nonsense, she dusted Bea with powder and played with her, kissing her tummy until she giggled and clutched at her mother's hair, and squealing so loud that Mary didn't hear Tyler until he cleared his throat and she spun round, her heart jerking frantically.

He was standing in the doorway, tall and solid and somehow definite, and all the air seemed to have whooshed from her lungs as she sat back on her heels, one hand to her throat.

'Hi,' she said, and her voice sounded abnormally high. 'I didn't realise you were back.'

'Sorry, I didn't mean to startle you.'

Tyler felt lumbering and awkward hanging around in the doorway, but he was reluctant to intrude into the happy scene in the bathroom. Mary's back had been to the door and he had watched her laughing with her baby, moved in a way he couldn't quite identify. She was pink and flushed still, her hair all messy where Bea had been clutching it in her tiny fists.

'That's all right. I just wasn't expecting you back yet,' she said. 'You're early tonight.'

'I thought I should follow up on lesson one,' said Tyler, 'and spend more time at home now you're here.'

It was impossible not to feel pleased, even though she knew that he was just playing a part.

'Very good,' she approved. 'We'll have to teach you about communication next. An email or a text during the day would be just the thing to let me know that you're thinking of me!'

Tyler was still trying to decide if she was joking or not when a phone started ringing in the other room.

Mary got to her feet, brushing baby powder from her hands. 'That's my mobile. It'll be my mother. I'm hoping she'll be able to look after Bea for me tomorrow.' She glanced from the baby to him and hesitated. 'Would you mind keeping an eye on her for a second while I answer it?'

'Er…all right.'

Left alone with the baby, Tyler was conscious of a moment of panic. Bea didn't like being abandoned by her mother and her small face darkened ominously. Terrified that she was going to cry, Tyler moved into the room and squatted down beside her on the floor.

They eyed each other dubiously. Tyler couldn't remember being this close to a baby before and he studied her with a kind of reluctant fascination. She was perfect in miniature, he thought, with ten tiny fingers and ten tiny toes. When he stretched out his hand tentatively, she clutched at his finger with surprising strength, a determined look on her face.

She had a round little tummy, chubby legs and plump arms that ended in a fold at the wrist, and her round eyes were not only the same luminous grey as her mother's but seemed to Tyler to hold an identically critical expression.

Ridiculously nervous, he tried a smile but that seemed to be a mistake. Bea's expression changed and for an appalling moment he thought she was going to burst into tears.

'No, no, don't do that,' he said hastily and tried to distract her by reaching out to prod her tummy.

To his huge relief, the stormy look vanished from her eyes and she dissolved into one of her gummy smiles instead. Encouraged, Tyler tried it again and she chuckled, so he tickled her feet next, making her giggle and try to grab her toes.

'One step, two steps…' he began, his fingers marching up her arm. It was obviously a game that she recognised because she squealed with excitement. She was enjoying herself so much that Tyler couldn't help laughing.

'She likes you,' Mary said from behind him, and Tyler turned to see her watching them with a curious expression in her eyes.

Feeling a fool, he got to his feet. 'I thought she

was going to cry,' he said to explain the uncharacteristic lapse into playfulness.

'She looks pretty happy to me,' said Mary, moving into the bathroom, and Tyler caught a waft of her perfume as she passed.

She knelt down next to the baby and reached for a nappy. 'Did you like playing with Tyler?' she asked Bea, who chortled and waved her arms and shouted.

Mary laughed and Tyler felt an odd tightening in his chest as she looked up at him.

'I think that means yes!' she said.

CHAPTER SIX

HE COULD go now. He had done his bit coming to say hello, but something held Tyler in the warm, light bathroom.

Mary glanced at him. 'Would you like to have a go at putting on a nappy?' she asked, and suppressed a smile at his visible recoil.

'No, thank you!'

'It would be very good practice for you,' she pointed out. 'You're the one who wants to have a family, so you might as well get used to babies.'

'I'm not changing a nappy,' he said firmly, but he was watching as Mary fastened Bea's nappy and deftly buttoned her into a Babygro.

'You know, being good with babies is a very attractive trait in a man,' she teased. 'It would be a big plus when you've found the woman of your dreams and are trying to impress her.'

'I'm hoping that the woman of my dreams will be more impressed by where Watts Holdings figures in the Dow Jones Index,' said Tyler austerely

'But think how handy the experience will be when you have children of your own!'

'I won't be changing their nappies,' he said, half suspecting that she was making fun of him and eyeing her suspiciously. 'I'll be at the office, working to support them.'

'Well, it's your loss,' said Mary, picking Bea up. 'They're gorgeous at this age. Why would you want to miss out on this?'

Holding Bea above her head, she blew raspberries against the baby's stomach. Convulsed with laughter, Bea grabbed at her hair.

'Ouch!' said Mary playfully and brought the baby back to her shoulder for a cuddle, kissing her downy head as Bea bumped her forehead against her mother's nose.

'Show Tyler how well you can kiss,' Mary said, laughing, and Bea banged her open mouth against Mary's.

Mary melted the way she always did, and hugged her little daughter to her. 'You won't want to be in the office when you have children, Tyler,' she said. 'You'll be lost the moment your baby gives you a slobbery kiss like that.'

Tyler couldn't imagine it. He had been holding on to the idea of a wife and family, but he hadn't considered the reality of it. He hadn't thought about nappies or slobbery kisses or baby chuckles. What would it be like to have his own child? he wondered. The thought kindled a tiny glow deep inside him.

The tight feeling in his chest wouldn't go away. Tyler badly wanted to think that it was irritation, but he was very much afraid that it might be jealousy. He wasn't jealous of the baby—Good Lord, how pathetic would that be? Just because all Bea had to do was stretch out her arms and Mary was there, to pick her up and kiss her and cuddle her! Of course he wasn't *jealous*.

Or maybe he was a little bit jealous, but only of the bond between Mary and her daughter. He was prepared to accept that he might feel that. He could see how completely they loved each other, how openly they laughed and kissed, how easy it was for them to show tenderness. Tyler recognised it as love, but it wasn't an emotion he had ever felt, and he didn't think that he ever would.

He looked away. 'Is she going to bed now?'

'Not yet. She needs some supper first.' Hoisting Bea up, Mary got to her feet. 'I got some shopping in the market today, so I'm going to make us a meal too. You did say that it was all right, and I think Mrs Palmer's grateful for the break.'

'Fine by me,' said Tyler, still feeling awkward and uneasy for some reason. 'Thank you.'

'When would you like to eat?'

He opened his mouth to reply before remem-

bering his lesson from the night before. 'When
would suit you?'

Mary laughed. 'You're a quick learner, I'll give
you that! Would eight o'clock be too early for you?'

'Eight's fine.'

'I'm just going to be putting Bea to bed and pot-
tering around until then if you want to do some
work,' she said.

'Oh. Right.' It sounded like a dismissal to Tyler.
'Good,' he said and cleared his throat. 'I'll be in my
study then.'

Tyler switched off the phone and tossed it on to his
desk. There was a whole pile of papers waiting for
his attention and he reached for the first one before
dropping it back with an irritable sigh.

This was ridiculous. It had been hard enough
trying to concentrate last night, but tonight was even
worse, and the slow tick of the clock on the mantel-
piece only emphasised the silence.

He wondered where Mary was. In the kitchen
probably, he thought, humming away and chatting
to Bea, filling the room with warmth and light and
laughter.

He could go and see what she was doing. The
thought lodged in Tyler's brain, unsettling him, and
he drummed his fingers on the desktop uncertainly.
There was no need for him to find her. She wasn't
a guest, and anyway she probably wanted time on

her own. And it wasn't as if he didn't have plenty of work to do here.

On the other hand, he realised, it would be thoughtful to go and see if she needed anything. He could offer to make her a cup of tea or something. *Imagine you're in love with me,* she had said. He was supposed to remember to be attentive for the next time he brought a real girlfriend here.

Tyler tried to picture his next girlfriend. She would be tall and willowy, probably, because that was the kind of woman he found attractive. She would be sensible and well-groomed and she wouldn't clutter up his house with baby paraphernalia, or tick him off for not paying her enough attention or tease him about changing nappies. She would be sweet-natured and beautiful and…

Boring? a subversive voice in his head suggested before Tyler could stamp down on it.

Nice, he substituted instead.

She would be perfect.

And, in the meantime, he might as well work on his relationship skills. He could go and find Mary with a clear conscience. Pushing back his chair, Tyler got to his feet.

He found her, as predicted, in the kitchen. Bea was banging a spoon on the tray of her high chair and shouting while Mary tasted a spoonful of her supper to check the temperature.

'All right, all right, I'm coming,' she said to Bea,

pulling out a chair with her foot. Catching sight of Tyler, she grimaced. 'I wouldn't come in unless you've got a strong stomach! Bea loves her food, but watching her eat isn't a pretty sight!'

'I'll risk it,' said Tyler. He watched her scoop up a spoonful of purée and offer it to Bea, who grabbed the spoon with both hands and proceeded to smear it over her face. He saw what Mary meant now.

Averting his eyes, he went over to the kettle. 'I was going to make a cup of tea,' he said stiltedly. 'Would you like one? Or something stronger?'

Mary would have killed for a gin and tonic just then, but it wasn't quite six yet and she had downed half a bottle of wine in double-quick time last night. She didn't want Tyler thinking that she had no control.

'Tea would be lovely,' she said.

She studied him under her lashes as she fed Bea. He was leaning back against the counter, legs crossed at the ankle and arms folded, while he waited for the kettle to boil. He'd rolled up his sleeves and loosened his tie, but somehow those signs of relaxation only served to make him seem tougher and more formidable than ever.

He was so solid, so self-contained, so *definite*, thought Mary. She always felt as if she was unravelling at the edges, but there was a steadiness to him that was insensibly reassuring. You felt as if you could hold on to him and be safe, no matter what else was happening.

And now she knew how it felt to hold on to him, the image was impossible to dislodge. She remembered the hardness of his body, the strength of his arms, the sureness of his lips, so that she only had to look at him, like now, and feel the heat flare through her, rushing along her veins and flushing her skin and tying her entrails into knots.

Gulping, she concentrated fiercely on loading another spoonful of purée for Bea.

'What *is* that?' Tyler asked with distaste.

'Chicken with carrot and leek.'

'It looks disgusting!'

'Oh, dear, and I made extra for you specially. *Now* what are we going to eat tonight?' Mary was doing her best to keep a straight face, but Tyler could see the corner of her mouth twitching.

'Right,' he said, and then he smiled that smile that made Mary's stomach do a spectacular somersault and land again like a fat quivering jelly. That didn't feel quite so damn funny.

Unaware of the effect of a single grin, Tyler nodded in Bea's direction. 'She seems to be enjoying it, anyway.'

Mary was glad of the excuse to look at her daughter instead. Bea was a messy eater, even allowing for the fact that she was only seven months old. Purée was liberally daubed over her face and there were bits of carrot and chicken stuck in her hair, up her nose and over her ears, and she chortled as she busily smeared any droppings over her tray.

'It'll be a while before we can take her to tea at the Ritz,' she agreed. 'I'm hoping she'll sleep after this. She's had a busy day.'

The kettle had boiled and Tyler turned to pour water into two mugs. 'Did you take her to the office with you?'

'Yes, she was really good.' Mary scraped the bowl for Bea. 'I just hope she'll be as good tomorrow.'

'Why, what's happening then?'

'I've got a meeting with Steven Halliday at eleven to talk about the new contract. I'd been hoping to leave her with Mum, but I don't think I can ask her now.'

'Was that her on the phone earlier?'

'Yes, but she's preoccupied with sorting out things with Bill at the moment, and she said something about meeting him tomorrow. I don't want to complicate things by mentioning Bea, because I know she'd say yes, and I think she needs to concentrate on herself at the moment.' Mary shrugged as she got up to rinse the bowl in the sink. 'I'll just have to take her with me.'

Tyler was holding the milk over her mug, his brows raised in query, and she nodded. 'Thanks,' she said, and smiled at him as she took the mug. 'Do you think Steven will mind?'

'Not if I tell him not to,' he said.

'You can't do that!'

Tyler lifted his brows. 'I can do what I like,' he said with a return to his old arrogance. 'It's my company.'

'Well, yes, but your employees *are* the company. You've got to take their feelings into account.'

'It's a business, Mary. The only thing I have to take into account is profits. If Steven doesn't like the way I run the company, he can go and work elsewhere. I don't see any reason for him to object to Bea's presence, but you might find it difficult to concentrate on the meeting yourself if she's there.'

'That's true.' Mary bit her lip worriedly. 'I've left it a bit late to ring any of my friends, though.'

'Someone in the office will be able to look after her for an hour or so,' said Tyler. 'I'll ask Carol. She's my PA and, before you say anything, no, I don't think she'll mind.'

'I think *I'd* mind if somebody dumped a baby on me without warning when I was trying to work,' said Mary doubtfully. 'Well, I'll see how it goes. With any luck Bea'll sleep through the whole meeting and I won't need to ask anyone to look after her.'

But at five to eleven the next morning, Bea was wide awake. She had slept in the car on the way in and was looking refreshed and alert and not in the least in need of a restorative nap any time soon.

'Typical,' Mary said to her with a sigh.

She couldn't help remembering the last time she

had been in the Watts Building, when her shoes had been killing her and Tyler had come up with the preposterous suggestion that she do a bit of relationship coaching on the side.

It seemed a very long time ago now. Mary was finding it hard to reconcile the ruthless businessman she had met then with the Tyler who had squatted down by her daughter and tickled her tummy until she laughed. She hadn't even liked him when she'd met him then and now... Mary didn't want to analyse too closely exactly what she felt now. All she knew was that her entrails jerked themselves into a knot every time she saw him.

She had been careful to wear more sensible shoes this time, and it made walking on the floor a lot easier. Without the crowds of people, the foyer seemed vast and impressive.

The receptionist looked askance at Bea, but promised to let Steven Halliday know that she was waiting. Mary carried Bea over to the glass wall that ran along the riverfront and pointed out a solitary rower sculling past.

It was a still, bright day and the river was like a mirror, reflecting the range of buildings that lined its banks, representing centuries of development from the medieval Guildhall to contemporary bars with their glass walls and decking. Amongst them all, the Watts Building stood out. It made no concessions to its historic backdrop. It didn't try to blend in with its neighbours, but demanded that you took it on its own terms.

A bit like Tyler, in fact.

'Mary?' A man in a suit was coming towards her, his hand outstretched. 'I'm Steven Halliday. How nice to meet you.'

Mary shook his hand mechanically, but her attention was riveted on the man beside him, a man whose appearance had made her heart lurch into her throat and lodge there, hammering frantically.

'I didn't know that you were going to be in on the meeting,' she blurted out, and then felt stupid.

'I'm not,' said Tyler calmly. 'I came to see if Bea was sleeping, and if not to see whether you'd like me to find someone to look after her.'

As Bea had recognised Tyler and was holding her arms out towards him with a crow of delight, there seemed no point in pretending that she was on the point of falling asleep. Meekly, Mary found herself handing her daughter over to him.

Their hands brushed as Bea was passed over, and Mary was mortified to feel the colour rise in her cheeks.

'Thank you,' she said stiffly. 'But if your PA is busy, will you promise to bring her back to me?'

'I'm sure it won't be necessary.' Tyler looked at Bea, who beamed back and fastened her little fingers around his nose, making him wince. 'Do you want to come with me, Miss Thomas?'

'Ba!'

Bea let herself be carried off without a backward look at her mother.

Mary couldn't help thinking that having Bea with her might have been less disturbing in the long run than Tyler's intervention, but was going to have to think about that later. For now she had a meeting to attend.

In the end, her discussion with Steven Halliday was extremely productive. Steven himself was not exactly obsequious, but he clearly thought she had a much closer relationship with Tyler than was in fact the case. Mary couldn't tell him that she was just providing a service like any other consultant without betraying Tyler's confidence and, anyway, he wasn't likely to believe her, having seen his boss so obviously at home with her baby.

At the end of the meeting, Steven escorted her personally to Tyler's office on the top floor with a fantastic view over the city. Carol, his PA, was a cool and elegant blonde who immediately made Mary feel fat and crumpled, but she smiled from behind her desk.

'Are you looking for Bea?' she asked.

'Yes.' Mary looked around the pristine office. 'I was rather expecting her to be with you. Is she here?'

For answer, Carol put a finger to her lips and walked over to a door, opening it noiselessly and beckoning Mary over. Through the open door, they watched Tyler pacing around his office, Bea in one arm and a report in his free hand.

'Five billion sounds excessive to me. What do you think?' he was saying.

'Ga! Ba ba ga!' said Bea and he nodded with apparent seriousness.

'I couldn't agree with you more. But the environmental impact assessment sounds promising, eh?'

'Ya!' shouted Bea, pulling at his earlobes with her small fingers.

Mary and Carol exchanged a look. 'He cancelled two meetings,' whispered Carol. 'He's had her the whole time. I think he's smitten!'

Mary's answering smile was just a little bit tight as she knocked on the door to attract Tyler's attention. Uh-oh, she thought, appalled at her reaction. It smacked suspiciously of jealousy, and of her own daughter too!

'Am I interrupting?' she asked brightly. Too brightly.

'I was just trying to keep her amused,' said Tyler, sounding faintly defensive. He looked so guilty, and Bea looked so content, that Mary felt her sudden tension melt in a rush of warmth that was perilously close to tenderness, or even love, but which she decided in the end was affection.

Yes, affection. It was a good neutral word. She could legitimately feel affection for Tyler, even if he was a client, Mary decided. He had just spent the last couple of hours looking after her daughter. He could be a friend.

Just not a lover.

'Absolutely,' she agreed, straight-faced. 'Business plans do it for me every time too.'

Tyler shifted a little uncomfortably. 'I didn't have anything more interesting.'

'Bea doesn't care,' Mary reassured him, rather touched by the rare glimpse of uncertainty. Bea had squealed with delight at the sight of her mother and was clamouring for her notice, so Mary held out her arms as Tyler passed her back. 'She doesn't know what you're reading. All she wants is your attention and the sound of your voice. Don't you?' she added to Bea, tossing her in the air. 'How are you at analysing business plans, anyway?'

'She's been great,' said Tyler, trying, not that successfully, to disguise his disappointment at having to hand Bea back. 'She never criticises or argues back, and she thinks all my ideas are great. She's the perfect companion!' he added, unable to resist tickling her hand with his finger, which looked enormous in comparison.

Bea immediately put on a fit of shyness, burying her face in her mother's neck, but then spoilt the effect entirely by peeping a glance at him under her ridiculously long lashes, smiling and then hiding again as soon as he smiled back.

'Stop flirting,' Mary said to her with mock sternness, but she couldn't help laughing too, which was a mistake as her eyes met Tyler's in what was supposed to be shared amusement but which turned instead into something infinitely more disturbing as their smiles faded and the air tightened between them.

It was extraordinary how that pale glacier-blue gaze could burn into her and make her feel so…hot. Warmth was tingling through her and she was horribly afraid that Tyler would see the colour staining her cheeks, but when she tried to look away she found that she couldn't.

Snared in the blueness of his eyes, Mary felt the breath evaporating from her lungs and for a long, long moment she could only stare helplessly back at him while the silence spun round them until there was only the unsteady thump of her heart and the slow, shaky simmering in her veins.

And then, as if sensing that she had lost their attention, Bea squawked and batted her mother on the nose in a peremptory reminder of her priorities. Startled, Mary managed to jerk her eyes away from Tyler's and gulp a breath at the same time.

Swallowing, she wondered if she were capable of stringing a sentence together. 'Thank you for looking after her, anyway,' she said at last, squirming at how high and strained her voice sounded. 'It was very kind of you.'

Tyler made a dismissive gesture. 'Did you have

a successful meeting?' he asked after another awkward little pause.

'Very, thanks to you.'

The stilted politeness was awful.

Bea was clutching her hair and bumping her head against Mary's throat, which at least gave her an excuse to leave. Mary tilted her jaw out of head-butting range and produced another bright smile.

'I must take Bea out of your way and let you get on with some work,' she said. 'What time do you think you'll be back tonight?'

That sounded awfully domestic, she realised belatedly. 'I mean...obviously, just come back whenever you want,' she explained. 'We're fine without you.'

Oh, God, that didn't come out right either.

'That is, we'll just be doing our usual routine,' she tried again, miserably aware of the deepening colour in her cheeks.

Not that Tyler seemed to care. He was already turning back to his desk. 'I'll aim for about six,' he said indifferently.

Mary did her best to pretend that she was similarly indifferent but, in spite of all her efforts to the contrary, she ended up watching the clock as six o'clock approached. She rationed the number of times she could look but, no matter how long she tried to spin it out, barely a minute would have crawled past. Had something happened to the rotation of the earth? she wondered wildly. If time went any slower it would start going backwards, and then where would they be?

As long as it didn't rewind too far, it might not be a bad thing, Mary reflected. Say, to a week ago, when Tyler Watts had been no more than a fading memory of a demanding boss.

Having taken its time about getting there, six o'clock came and went in a blur with no sign of Tyler. In the kitchen, Mary was furious with herself for being so disappointed and set about chopping an onion with savage concentration. It was nearly half past by the time she heard the front door bang.

He was here. The realisation sucked the air out of Mary's lungs and she made herself inhale very slowly and very carefully. There was a sick butterfly feeling in her stomach and every nerve in her body seemed to be jangling and jitterbugging in a frenzy of awareness.

Oh, for heaven's sake, Mary told herself, exasperated at last. Pull yourself together!

'Sorry I'm late,' said Tyler, appearing at the kitchen door a few moments later. 'There was a bit of a crisis in the London office.'

'Not a problem,' said Mary brightly.

She was utterly horrified by how much she wished she could go over and lean against him. Where had it come from, this urge to feel his arms close around her, to lift her face for a kiss? She needed to get out of here—and quick.

'I'm just about to put her to bed,' she said, lifting Bea out of the high chair. 'Is eight o'clock OK for supper again?'

'Fine,' said Tyler, quelled by her brisk manner.

He had been looking forward to coming home all afternoon, and to sitting in the warm kitchen and watching her with Bea, but she seemed to be making it clear that his presence wasn't required, so he could hardly hang around.

'I'll go and do some work,' he said.

Wonderful smells were drifting from the kitchen when Tyler made his way along the stone-flagged hall at eight o'clock. Mary was there, slicing tomatoes and looking round and rosy in a red jumper and soft trousers, but her smile seemed to him to hold a hint of brittleness.

'Can I do anything?' he asked.

'No, it's fine. Supper's nearly ready.'

Mary had given herself another stern lecture while she'd been putting Bea to bed. She had to stop being silly and remember what she was doing here. Tyler was a client, and she needed to keep their relationship on a professional level. Yes, it was hard when they were living together like this, but that was the part of the job.

Moving in with him had been her idea, Mary reminded herself. She was getting very well paid for it and it was time to stop messing around and earn her five thousand pounds. And that meant not thinking about how nice it would feel to lean against him or wondering what it would be like if their relationship was real after all. It wasn't real. It was a pretence, and she had better not forget it.

'This is very different from what I'm used to,' said Tyler as she set the dishes on the table.

'What is?' she asked in surprise.

'All of this.' He gestured at the table. 'Sitting in the kitchen, eating home-cooked food…'

'What do you usually do with your girlfriends in the evening?' asked Mary, and then could have bitten her tongue out. What a stupid question! 'I mean, you know, when you're not…'

'Not what?' asked Tyler, raising an eyebrow.

'You know,' she said crossly.

They couldn't spend their whole time in bed, surely? But then maybe they did. A real girlfriend wouldn't be faffing around making tomato salad. She would be lying warm and naked beside Tyler, arching beneath him as his hands drifted and curved and demanded, shuddering luxuriously at the feel of his lips against her skin. Or she would be leaning over him, her hair tickling him as she explored the lean, hard body and found a way past the tough, driven exterior to the real man underneath.

'Ouch!' Mary burnt her finger on the roasting dish and sucked it furiously as she tried to steady her breath. Served her right for letting her imagination get carried away. She could really have done with a bucket of cold water, but the burn had done a good job of shocking her back to reality.

'I tend to take girlfriends out to eat,' Tyler answered her question at last. 'Mrs Palmer might leave a meal sometimes, I suppose, but we never did this.' He watched as Mary lifted the rack of lamb from the roasting dish and set it on a board, slicing it into chops, her burnt finger held at an awkward angle. 'I've never had food like this before.'

'What, you've never had roast lamb?'

'In a restaurant, or heated up in a microwave. Never cooked in the oven and then put on the table so you can all eat together.' Tyler couldn't explain how strange it felt. How strange and how nice.

Mary divided the lamb between two plates and set them on the table. 'Not even when you were growing up?' she asked. 'Didn't your mother cook for you?'

'She may have done. I certainly don't remember if she did. She died when I was six so my father brought me up.' Tyler's voice was quite expressionless. 'He wasn't what you'd call a domesticated man. He'd open a tin of beans or something occasionally, and he'd buy takeaways when he remembered about eating, but he would certainly never have dreamt of cooking a meal.'

Mary's heart ached for the little boy who had lost his mother. 'He didn't marry again?'

'No. I don't think he really wanted to get married the first time round, to tell you the truth. I suspect they only did it because my mother got pregnant, and it wasn't as easy to be a single mother then as it is now.'

'I wouldn't describe it as easy now,' said Mary ruefully, 'but I know what you mean.'

'He wasn't a particularly attentive father but, after my mother died, he was the only parent I had,' Tyler went on. 'I yearned for his approval, but he didn't give it easily. I'd take pictures for him home from school, but he'd just toss them aside and say they were scribbles and, looking back, I suppose that's exactly what they were.'

Mary flinched. She couldn't wait for Bea's first pictures. She would be proud of every scribble and stick them on the fridge for the world to admire. What had it been like for a lonely little boy to have his offerings tossed aside with contempt?

'But sometimes, if I did something really well, he would be pleased with me and a casual "good boy" from him was worth any amount of gold stars from a teacher,' Tyler confessed, his mouth twisted with self-mockery.

No wonder Tyler was so driven to succeed now, thought Mary. No wonder he found relationships so hard. He had never had one to use as a model. He had never seen that a man and a woman could live happily together and talk and laugh and love each other and be friends. He didn't know what it was to be unconditionally loved, so he didn't know how to love himself.

It explained a lot.

She wanted to reach out and hug him, to reach the little boy he had been, but she couldn't do that.

Because professionals don't hug their clients, do they, Mary?

CHAPTER SEVEN

MARY let Tyler pour her some wine instead. 'It must have been very lonely for you growing up.'

He shrugged. 'Maybe. It was normal for me, whatever it was.'

'I'm an only child too,' she offered. 'My father died when I was nine, but my experience was very different from yours. My mother was always loving, and she married again when I was twenty and had left home.'

'How did you feel about that?'

'I was a bit jealous at first,' she confessed. 'But when I saw her and Bill together, I realised how lonely she had been all those years. She deserved to be happy.'

'I'm not sure how I would have got on with a stepmother,' said Tyler. 'As it was, my father died when I was sixteen, and since then I haven't had to worry about what anyone else thinks. When you're only accountable to yourself, you can take risks you wouldn't otherwise be able to take. I built up my first company from scratch, made a million and lost everything, so then I had to start all over again. I wouldn't have been able to do that if I'd had to think about someone else.'

'You're going to have to think about someone else if you get married,' Mary pointed out.

'I suppose so.' Tyler didn't sound particularly enthused at the prospect. 'Not that my wife will be concerned with the business side of things.'

'Why not?' said Mary. 'You can't divide life into neat little compartments.' She could see his jaw setting mulishly, and she sighed. 'The whole point of marriage is that the two of you share everything,' she told him patiently. 'I'm not suggesting your wife is in on every business decision, but she'll certainly want to know if you're worried about work, just like you'll need to know if there's anything *she's* worried about. You're going to have to learn to talk to each other.'

'Why are women so obsessed with talking?' said Tyler with a return to his old irritability. 'All they ever say is, "We need to talk," when what they mean is, "I need to tell you what you're doing wrong"!'

Mary took a reflective slug of her wine. 'If you'd ever listened to what they had to say, you might not be in a position where you have to pay me five thousand pounds to say much the same thing,' she pointed out with deceptive mildness. 'Anyway, it's not just about discussing problems. You shouldn't marry anyone you're not happy just to sit and chat to, without ever having to think of something to say. A fulfilling relationship is about a lot more than sex, you know.'

'Are you suggesting that we don't have sex until we're married?' asked Tyler, lifting his brows derisively.

There was a short pause while they both listened to his words echoing into the silence.

'When I say "we", of course I don't mean you and me,' he added, his colour slightly heightened. 'I mean a future fiancée.'

'Of course,' said Mary, pleased to be the one who could sound smooth and understanding for once. 'I'd certainly agree that sex is an important part of most relationships, but when you do meet someone, you should bear in mind that she's not likely to consider marrying you if she thinks that you're only interested in her for sex.'

There, listen to her talking coolly to Tyler about sex. She sounded positively professional.

It was just a pity she didn't *feel* cool and professional.

'So you suggest that I spend the evenings sitting and talking to her instead?'

'There are worse ways to spend an evening,' said Mary dryly, but Tyler was unconvinced.

'I should think it would get pretty boring,' he said, firmly suppressing the realisation that he hadn't been bored at all sitting and talking to Mary.

'It's not boring if you're with someone you love,' she was saying, her words overlapping his thought with an unintentionally disturbing effect. 'No, don't roll your eyes,' she went on as he did his best to disguise his reaction. 'I'm serious.'

'Is this the old you-should-only-marry-for-love argument, by any chance?' he asked, leaning over the table to refill her wineglass.

Mary's lips thinned. 'You seem to think that marriage is something you can acquire, like a car or a boat,' she said. 'It's not like that. It isn't about having a wife you can show off to your friends. It's about being with the one person who can light up your life and make you feel better just being near her, and she needs to feel the same way about you.'

'Is that how you felt about Alan?' he asked, his voice hard, and she looked away.

'Yes,' she said sadly. 'It was like that and it didn't last, but that doesn't mean I don't believe that what I'm saying is true. Your wife, whoever she is, shouldn't just be that. She needs to be your rock, your anchor, the only one who can make the rest of your life make sense. When you find someone like that, Tyler, then *that's* when you should get married, because you'll know in your heart that she's the one.'

'But what if she's *not* the one?' he argued. The idea of Alan being the one who lit up Mary's life was annoying, like an itchy little insect bite. 'It's all very well saying you'll know, but people change. They fall out of love as easy as they fall into it. You only have to look at the statistics for divorce nowadays to realise that. Sometimes they don't even make it as far as the altar. Look at you and Alan,' he said, which perhaps wasn't fair, but he wasn't feeling particularly fair this evening.

Mary winced, but she met his gaze squarely. 'It's true that my relationship with Alan didn't work out,' she said quietly, 'but it wasn't because we fell out of love. It was because we couldn't find a compromise when it came to having a baby.'

She paused. 'My experience only proves the point I'm trying to make, which is that if you want a successful relationship—and you say you do—then you both have to be prepared to work at it and learn to compromise. If you don't, then chances are that you'll end up as a statistic like me, and I'm sure you don't want that.'

Tyler didn't. He wasn't prepared to contemplate the prospect of failure on any front.

He drained his glass and set it down on the table. 'If it's going to be that hard work, I think I'd rather skip the whole lighting up my life bit,' he said with an air of finality. 'My marriage is much more likely to succeed if I choose someone with the same practical approach as mine.'

'Well, OK, if that's your attitude,' said Mary, giving up with a shrug.

It was almost a relief to be reminded of Tyler's

cold-blooded approach to marriage, she reflected. There had been times when he had come perilously closely to seeming like the kind of man it would be all too easy to fall in love with, she had to admit. When he smiled at Bea, or held her in his big square hands, she was in danger of forgetting that he was also a man who focused ruthlessly on his goal.

Right now, his goal was to get married and he certainly wasn't thinking of a woman like her. And that was just as well, Mary reminded herself. Her heart was still raw from Alan's rejection and the last thing she needed was to get involved with a man like Tyler who didn't believe in love and wanted very different things out of life. Her job was to help him make a success of a relationship with someone else entirely.

'In that case, though, it's even more important to make sure that you've found the right woman and spend time getting to know her rather than just falling into bed, isn't it?' she said in resolutely professional mode. 'Remember, you're going to be spending the rest of your life together, so if you've used up all your conversation on the first date, that's not going to be a good sign. Surely you want to marry someone who's going to be a good companion over the years, who's interesting and intelligent and doesn't bore you?'

'Of course I do,' said Tyler, although he couldn't think of a single woman he knew who fitted that particular bill. Except Mary, of course, and he had already decided that she wasn't the kind of wife he wanted.

'You're going to have to work hard to convince an interesting, intelligent woman that the kind of marriage you've got in mind is one that she might want,' Mary warned, and he scowled.

'That's what you're here for,' he reminded her.

Quite. Better not forget that, Mary.

Pushing back her chair, she gathered the empty plates and carried them across to the dishwasher. 'Talking of why I'm here, it's time to move on to your next lesson,' she said brightly.

'*Another* one?'

'You've only had three!' she pointed out. 'The first one was about the importance of compromising,' she went on, counting them off on her fingers. 'The second was about making a prospective wife feel welcome and wanted and the third was showing that you can be good with babies. I'd have to give you full marks on that one after the way you looked after Bea this morning,' she finished.

'So what's lesson four?'

'Communication,' said Mary succinctly.

'Communication?'

'See? You don't even know what communication is!'

'Of course I do,' snapped Tyler. 'I just don't—'

'Understand why it's so important in a relationship?'

'No,' he said, gritting his teeth. 'I was going to say, before you interrupted me, that I don't see the difference between communication and talking, and we've already done that.'

Mary set a plum tart on the table and went to the fridge for some cream. She shouldn't really, but she had already had half a packet of biscuits today, so it was a bit late to worry about the diet. She would start that tomorrow.

'They're related, of course,' she told Tyler, 'but I'm thinking about communication more as keeping in touch. With your previous girlfriends, did you ring them during the day at all?'

'Not when I'm at work,' he said, sounding appalled at the very idea.

'Did you send emails, perhaps? A text now and then?'

'I go to the office to work,' said Tyler pointedly, 'not waste my time on personal calls.'

Mary tutted as she sat back down at the table. 'Right, so you're a compartment man. You close the door in the morning when you leave the house and put all thought of everything except work out of your mind until you get home again at night.'

'How else am I supposed to concentrate on my business?' demanded Tyler, remembering uncomfortably how hard he had found it to put Mary out of his mind today. 'I like to focus on one thing at a time.'

That figured, thought Mary. 'I can see multi-tasking isn't your strong suit,' she said, cutting him a slice of the tart, 'but you can't run a relationship like a business, whatever you think. When you're building a relationship with a woman, you want to make her feel that she's special, and you can do that by making contact when you're apart during the day.'

'I can't spend all day on the phone,' he said irritably. 'I'd never get anything done.'

'I'm not suggesting long conversations, but a spontaneous call to let her know that you're thinking about her would make a big difference. You don't have to talk for long.'

Tyler had his stubborn look on, she saw. 'Look,' she said, 'what have we just been saying about having to work hard if you want the right woman? It's not that difficult to send a text, is it? And an email only takes a few seconds. What's the problem?'

'I wouldn't know what to say,' he admitted grudgingly.

'Just say "I'm thinking about you", "I miss you"… You could even go the whole hog and say "I love you",' said Mary, and then stopped. 'Oh, except you aren't going to do love, are you?' she said, not without a touch of sarcasm. 'Scrap that one. "I like you" or "I respect you" don't have quite the same ring to them, so I'd avoid them too, but otherwise I don't think it matters what you say. It's just a way of letting her know that she's part of your life.'

She poured cream over her tart. 'I'll give you my mobile number and you can send me a text tomorrow,' she told him. 'It'll be good for you to get in the habit of it so, by the time you meet someone, you can do all this sort of thing as second nature. I'd better have your number too,' she added, pointing inelegantly with her spoon, her mouth full of tart.

'What for?' asked Tyler.

Mary swallowed her mouthful. 'I might need it,' she said. 'I might want you to pick up some extra milk on your way home or something.'

He bristled. 'I'm not a shopping service!'

'We're living together to all intents and purposes,' she said. 'The idea was that we do everything normal couples do.'

'Except sleep together,' said Tyler, and she flashed him a startled glance before dropping her eyes back to her plate.

'Except that,' she agreed.

'Mr Watts?'

'Hmm…what?' Startled out of his reverie, Tyler jerked round to see his PA standing in the doorway, watching him with a curious expression. 'What is it, Carol?' he asked gruffly, disliking being caught at a disadvantage.

'Are you ready for your eleven-thirty meeting?'

Meeting? What meeting? Tyler felt oddly disorientated this morning. Instead of working, he had spent the last twenty minutes spinning mindlessly in his chair, drumming his fingers on the leather arm and wishing he could get Mary's face out of his mind.

The thought of her had been distracting him all morning, and his two earlier meetings had been positively embarrassing. Tyler had seen the furtive glances the others around the table had exchanged on more than one occasion when he had had to have his attention recalled. He was famous for his sharpness and his focus, but both seemed to have deserted him today.

Tyler couldn't understand it. It wasn't as if Mary was beautiful. She wasn't even that pretty. The grey eyes were lovely, but her mouth was too wide, her nose too big and her chin too stubborn. As for those quirky eyebrows, they were plain odd. Somehow, though, the humour and intelligence in her face meant that you didn't really notice her features, and the more Tyler looked at her, the more he found himself deciding that she was really very attractive.

You want an interesting, intelligent woman, she had told him, and Tyler agreed. What he wanted was a woman like Mary, in fact, but without a baby or those ridiculously sentimental notions of love and marriage.

He wanted someone better groomed too, he reminded himself. Mary always seemed to be spilling out of her clothes and, if she was wearing something nice, ten to one she would have dropped something down her front. She was clumsy and critical and she had a sharp tongue. She was the last kind of woman he wanted to marry.

It was just that he liked watching her talk, liked watching the way her expressive face lit up as she gesticulated, liked the gleam of fun in her smile and the way she could keep her expression perfectly straight sometimes while her eyes brimmed with laughter.

'Mr Watts?' Carol prompted him. 'Is everything all right?'

'Of course,' snapped Tyler, humiliated by the open curiosity in her stare, and more than a little embarrassed at having been caught with his thoughts drifting yet again. 'Send them in—no, wait!' He changed his mind at the last moment. 'Give me five minutes.'

Carol nodded an acknowledgement and withdrew, closing the door carefully behind her as if humouring an eccentric, and Tyler was left alone. He picked up his mobile from his desk and then put it down again, staring at it as if it were a strange and unpredictable beast.

This was silly. He didn't do texting or schmaltzy emails, and he didn't want to start now. He was too old and too busy for that kind of thing.

On the other hand, it would only take a minute and if it made the difference Mary said it did, it was a technique he could—perhaps should—learn.

Abruptly, he picked up the phone and, using his thumb, typed in 'thinking about you', which was true, after all. He signed it T and, after a moment's hesitation, put an X after it. He wasn't completely clueless, whatever Mary thought. Then he pressed 'send' before he could change his mind.

'That was all that was required,' said Mary approvingly that evening when he got home. 'It wasn't so hard, was it?'

The hard bit had been waiting for her to reply. God knew what had gone on in that meeting! Tyler had spent the whole time trying not look at the phone, and when it had finally lit up to indicate that a message had been received it had been all he could do not to snatch it up. It had taken immense willpower to wait until he had hustled the meeting to a close before he'd let himself read her reply.

Ridiculously, he had even been conscious of a tiny thrill when he'd seen that it was indeed from Mary, although as a message it was hardly one to treasure. 'V good' she had written. 'Go to top of class. M XX'

The worst thing was that he had actually counted how many x's she had included. Tyler couldn't believe that he had actually noticed, let alone wondered what they had meant. Were two 'X's the equivalent of flirting?

Not that there was anything remotely flirtatious about Mary's manner when he got home. He had managed to leave the office by six again, and even the security guard had commented on his changed routine.

'You're not usually out of here much before nine, Mr Watts. There isn't a problem, is there?'

No, there wasn't a problem, Tyler reassured himself. There was just…Mary. And she was just doing what he had asked her to do. What he was *paying* her to do. There was no reason for him to feel that everything was changing. He was exactly the same as he had ever been. He was just applying himself to his course.

He sat in the kitchen with Bea on his lap, watching Mary cook while the baby explored his face with inquisitive little fingers, tugging at his lips and twisting his ears curiously.

'What's the lesson tonight?' he asked, wincing at a pinch. Those little fingers could give quite a nip.

'I've been thinking about that.' Mary turned from the worktop and wiped her hands on her apron. 'Keeping in touch the way you did today is good, but you also need to think about other ways you can show that you're aware of her needs.'

'Couldn't you be a bit more specific?' said Tyler, lost already.

Mary chewed a thumb absently as she tried to think of a way to explain. 'It's about being thoughtful and sensitive and putting yourself in her shoes,' she tried slowly. 'Maybe one day she'll need some comforting, and another one she'll want you to boost her confidence. Or she might want to be surprised.'

It all sounded very vague to Tyler, and he said so.

'Most women just want to feel loved and desired and appreciated,' said Mary. 'OK, so you're not going to make her feel loved, but you can at least try not to take her for granted. Don't get so wrapped up in your work that you forget to tell her that she's beautiful, or how much she means to you.'

'Right,' said Tyler, filing all this away. 'I'll try to be more thoughtful.'

Looking back later, Mary was surprised at how quickly she got used to living with Tyler. It was odd the way she could be so uncomfortably aware of him, and yet feel so comfortable when they were together. Most of the time, she had herself under pretty good control, and then it seemed perfectly natural that she should be living in a mansion or sitting at the kitchen table telling Tyler Watts, of all people, about her day.

But there were other times when it wasn't so easy. She would look at him tossing Bea into the air and her entrails would tangle themselves into a knot that left her feeling hollow and slightly sick. Or her eyes would get stuck on his hands or the crease in his cheeks and a wave of heat would catch her unawares, pushing the air from her lungs and setting her senses afire.

Mary couldn't understand it. True to his word, Tyler was trying to be thoughtful, but clearly it didn't come easily, and most of the time he reverted to his usual abrupt manner. He was brusque, impatient and irritable, with a sardonic turn of phrase and no charm whatsoever. There was absolutely no reason to feel breathless and giddy whenever he walked into the room.

But she still did.

Bea adored him. She crowed with delight when he walked in, and Tyler kept most of his rare smiles for her. Without either of them being quite aware how it happened, they fell into a routine where he fed Bea while Mary cooked supper. Mary would watch him out of the corner of her eye and marvel that the tough businessman she knew could be so patient and gentle with a baby. He managed to remain immaculate too. When she fed Bea she ended up with half her supper down her front, but Tyler sat fastidiously at arm's length and never got so much as a drop on his expensive Italian suit.

When Bea was thoroughly wiped down she was allowed to sit on his lap, which she loved, and if she was crying he grew quite adept at distracting her, walking around the room with her in his arms or tickling her until she giggled. He drew the line at changing a nappy, though, which Mary supposed was fair enough. Bea wasn't his baby, although sometimes it was hard to remember that.

Once Bea was in bed, they would have supper together and Mary found herself looking forward to that time with him far more than she ought. It was all too easy to forget that she was supposed to be a coach and he the client. Every now and then, one or other of them would recall that they should be discussing relationships, but usually they just talked.

They disagreed on most things, and as often as not they would end up arguing, but Mary even enjoyed that. Their arguments were always stimulating and she felt mentally alert in a way she hadn't done since Bea's birth. For the first few months as a mother, she had been consumed by worry: about Bea and Alan's attitude to her, about money and her mother, about finding somewhere to live and getting the agency off the ground and just getting through from one day to the next.

Those worries hadn't disappeared, but for the first time Mary felt able to shelve them for a while. She couldn't think about Alan or the need to find somewhere to live just yet. This month with Tyler felt like a time out of time. She was content to live for the moment, and if she was conscious of feeling more vibrant and alive than she ever had before, Mary chose not to question too closely why that should be.

So the arguments were fine. The times when they ended up laughing together were altogether more disturbing. Mary would lie awake those nights, tossing restlessly while Tyler's smile burned behind her eyelids, and remind herself that there was no point in liking him, let alone loving him.

She had absolutely no reason to suppose that he had changed his hard-headed attitude to marriage, or changed his mind in the slightest about the kind of woman he wanted for his wife. He had brought her flowers once, and he sent the odd email, but only when he remembered that he was supposed to be thoughtful. None of them meant anything. Lovely though they had been, the flowers weren't for her. They were just practice.

Tyler was very careful about touching her, she had noticed, and avoided where he could even a mere brush of their hands. It was usually he who ended their supper-time conversations. He would get up—often quite abruptly—and shut himself up in his study to work. It was clear that he had no interest in spending the whole evening with her, no matter how easily they had been talking.

And why should he? Mary asked herself bleakly. Face it, she was fat and frumpy and clumsy and untidy and probably boring too. Her life revolved around Bea and the agency, and she had no energy for anything else. She had spent an evening with her mother, and had been for a drink with an old school friend, but it wasn't exactly a high old social life. Glamourpuss she would never be. There was no use in fooling herself. She just wasn't the kind of woman Tyler wanted to show off to his peers, and that was all there was to it.

Not that she should care, Mary reminded herself, but it was getting harder and harder to remember why not.

The fine weather lasted for over two weeks until one morning Mary woke to gusty rain splattering against the windows. She dragged herself out of bed, rubbing her eyes wearily. It hadn't been a good night. Bea seemed to have picked up a cold from somewhere, and Mary had been up with her four times.

Bea's screams had woken Tyler too. At one point he had appeared bleary-eyed in the bedroom door and asked if he could help.

Bea had just been sick all over her, and you would have thought that she would have other things on her mind, but Mary had still found time to notice that he was wearing only a pair of pyjama bottoms. Tyler was always immaculately turned out and she had got used to seeing him in his pristine shirt and tie and his crisp suit. He looked very different in the middle of the night, with bare feet, a piratical stubble and his hair slightly tousled from his pillow.

Very different and very, very attractive.

His skin had looked smooth and warm and firm, and she could see the flex of muscles in his powerful shoulders. Impossible not to wonder what it would be like to reach out and lay the flat of her hand against his flank.

Mary had shivered at the thought. The dangerously enticing thought.

The shiver had been followed almost immediately by a wash of shame. What kind of mother was she? What other woman's pulse would kick up a notch at the sight of a broad, bare male chest when she had a sick child in her arms?

'I don't think there's anything you can do, but thanks anyway,' she said, firmly averting her eyes from him. 'Sorry we disturbed you.'

Tyler's unsettlingly pale gaze rested on her for a moment. 'I'll leave you to it, then,' he said abruptly, levering himself away from the doorframe and disappearing.

Probably horrified by the sight of her without her make-up on, thought Mary glumly as she cleaned Bea up and buttoned her into a fresh Babygro. Either that or he hadn't liked being scoped out by a middle-aged mum with piggy eyes and baby sick in her hair.

She was wearing her oldest, baggiest pyjamas too. They happened to be her most comfortable ones too, but they could hardly be said to be flattering. Mary felt enormous in them and, oh, look, the buttons down the front were all done up the wrong way too. *Not* a good look.

'Oh, well, what does it matter what I look like?'

Mary sighed to Bea, picking her up and cuddling her close. 'I'm never going to be slender and glamorous.'

Unlike Tyler's wife. She might not have a name yet, but Mary was quite sure that she would be the kind of woman who could look beautiful at four in the morning. Her hair would be blond and slightly dishevelled and she would look like an angel leaning over the cot in some seductive, slithery silk nightgown that Tyler wouldn't be able to keep his hands off and that would never, ever be stained by baby sick.

'Why should I care?' Mary demanded of her sleepy daughter.

There was no answer to that. Mary just knew that she did.

The miserable weather reflected Mary's spirits and she felt oppressed all day. There was no other reason to feel down, she kept reminding herself. Business was booming at the agency, her mother had finally settled things with Bill and was happier than Mary had seen her for a very long time, and she would be leaving Haysby Hall next week with five thousand pounds in her pocket. She could think about looking for a flat soon. She ought to be ecstatic.

The fact that she wasn't, Mary put down to the murky rain and the lowering grey cloud that squatted over the city. It had nothing to do with the prospect of leaving Tyler next week, she decided as she gave up on an unprofitable day early and headed home in the car. He probably couldn't wait for them to be gone, she thought drearily. Especially after last night.

Bea's mood was no better than Mary's. She was grizzling in the back seat and, between her and the frantic slap of the windscreen wipers, it took some time before Mary realised that the car was making funny noises.

To her dismay, it started coughing and steaming, until it spluttered to a halt a good five miles from Haysby Hall. Naturally, it picked the most isolated section of the narrow country road in which to stop.

Mary dropped her head on to the steering wheel and let out a long groan of despair. This was all she needed. The rain was driving against the windscreen and the wind buffeted the car and howled through the trees as if auditioning for Hammer House of Horrors.

In the back, Bea set up a wail, not liking the noise, and Mary gritted her teeth. There was no point in just sitting here. It was a struggle to push the door open into the wind, but she managed to get out and push the car further away from the dangerous bend, which was something.

By the time she got back into the car and switched on the hazard lights she was sodden through to her skin and she wiped the rain from her face. Now what? She had Bea's pushchair, but she couldn't walk her five miles in this. Thank heaven for mobiles. There was nothing for it but to ring for help.

Afterwards, Mary thought of all sorts of people

she could have called. Her mother was at home and could have arranged a taxi, or Bill would doubtless have come out to rescue her, but at the time she didn't even think. There was only one person whose voice she wanted to hear just then. She rang Tyler.

CHAPTER EIGHT

'WATTS,' Tyler barked into the phone, and just hearing him made Mary want to cry for some reason.

'It's me,' she said. 'Mary.'

'I'm in a meeting,' he said. 'What is it?'

'I've broken down in the middle of nowhere,' she said, fiercely swallowing the wobble in her voice. 'And I haven't got any cash. Can you ask Carol to get someone to come out and pick us up?'

Tyler didn't waste time on commiserations. He asked Mary where she was, told her to stay in the car until help came, and rang off.

Resigning herself to a miserable wait, Mary huddled in the back seat with Bea and tried not to think about how cold and wet she was, but it wasn't in the end that long before a knock on the window made her jump and she saw Tyler himself peering into the car under an umbrella.

'Come on, let's get you out of there,' he said.

Mary stared at him. 'I thought you were in a meeting,' was all she could think of to say.

'They're finishing it without me,' said Tyler. 'Hurry up, I'm getting wet out here,' he added when Mary just sat there as if stunned. 'And Bea looks as if she wants to go home, even if you don't.'

Chivvying her as if she were a recalcitrant child, Tyler got the two of them into his Porsche, which was wonderfully warm and dry. He took charge of her car, organised a mechanic to come and tow it away and then drove them home with a brisk competence that made Mary feel treacherously weepy. It was bliss to be looked after for once, to drop her head back against the leather seat and simply put herself in Tyler's capable hands.

She was dripping all over his luxurious leather upholstery and her wet clothes clung unpleasantly. 'I'm sorry about this,' she said as he put the car into gear and pulled out. 'I didn't mean to drag you out of your meeting.'

'It doesn't matter,' he said without looking at her.

He didn't seem to want to talk, but there was something so uncomfortable about the silence that Mary felt as if she had to persevere.

'You got here awfully quickly,' she said. 'You must have left straight away.'

He had, in fact, barely paused to make his excuses to the meeting, Tyler remembered. As soon as he had learnt that she was alone and in trouble, his one thought had been to get to her.

'There was no point in hanging around,' he said

tersely, not sure if he was cross with her for putting him in the situation where he abandoned meetings at the drop of a hat, or with himself for feeling so anxious until he had seen that she was safe.

The truth was that he had been irritable all day. He hadn't slept at all after Bea's crying had woken him in the middle of the night. He had lain in bed, unable to get the thought of Mary in those ridiculous pyjamas out of his mind. He could have understood if she had been spilling out of some sexy little number, but they had been faded and shabby and shapeless. And all he had been able to think about was how warm and lush she had looked, about how much he would have liked to be able to undo those buttons and lose himself in her luscious flesh and her soft curves, to—

But there Tyler pulled himself up short. The baby hadn't been well. Mary had been worried. It was downright perverse of him to be noticing how soft and warm and *touchable* she looked, with her brown hair all tousled and her grey eyes blurry with sleep.

Perverse and pointless. Mary, he reminded himself for the umpteenth time, had no part in his plans for the future. Thinking about what it would be like to make love to her was unprofitable, to say the least, and profitability always had to be the bottom line. He was a businessman, wasn't he?

It exasperated Tyler that somewhere along the line over the last three weeks he had lost his focus.

He was famous for his workaholic tendencies and for his ability to concentrate his energy on a single goal, but that had all gone by the board too. He couldn't work if Mary was in the house, no matter how firmly he shut himself up in his study, and he couldn't work if she was out either. One night she had gone to see her mother and the house had seemed cold and empty and lonely until she'd breezed back after ten.

Tyler felt as if he were losing control and it wasn't a feeling he liked. He was going to have to do something about it, he decided. Things couldn't go on like this. Mary was too distracting.

Look at her now. He glanced sideways to where she sat shivering in the passenger seat. Her hair was hanging in damp tendrils. Her nose was red. She looked wet and miserable and downright plain, but he felt a tightness in his chest that he couldn't explain just looking at her, and he was conscious of an absurd desire to stop the car, gather her into his arms and warm her with his body until she stopped shivering.

As it was, all he could do was reach forward and turn the heater on to full blast.

He had to get a grip, Tyler reminded himself fiercely. Keep an eye on his goal, remember his strategy. There was no reason why he shouldn't think of Mary as a friend, he decided, but not as anything more than that. That would be his new strategy, in fact.

That was his justification for sending her off to have a bath as soon as they got in, anyway. 'I'll look after Bea,' he said. 'You'd better get those wet clothes off.'

Mary sank into the bath with a long grateful sigh. The miserable day suddenly didn't seem quite so bad.

It was wonderful to feel warm again, but she had a nasty feeling that not all of the heat was due to the hot bath. There was a dangerous little glow inside her at the knowledge that Tyler had come to her rescue himself. He had even left a meeting early for her, which was unheard of in the history of Watts Holdings! He could easily have sent someone else, or had Carol sort out the whole sorry mess, but he had chosen to come himself. Mary hugged the knowledge to her.

Was this how all those fairy tale princesses felt when their knight galloped up on his charger? Tyler Watts made an unlikely knight, it had to be admitted. He was irascible rather than chivalrous, and he had been brusque and uncommunicative in the car, but that hadn't stopped her being agonisingly aware of him.

There was a solidity and a self-contained strength to him that was almost overwhelming at close quarters. His brows might be drawn forbiddingly across his nose, and his mouth might be set in a grimmer than usual line, but his stern presence was incredibly reassuring.

Mary had been seized by an almost uncontrollable desire to reach out and touch him. He had been so close. It would have been so easy to lay a hand on his thigh, to lean across and press her lips to his throat, to cling to that hard body. The urge had been so strong that her fingers had twitched and tingled, and she had clasped them in her lap, her heart hammering madly in her throat at the very thought of it.

She wouldn't have done it, of course. Having a lustful woman crawling all over him would have been far too distracting for Tyler when he was driving.

Wrong reason. Mary sat up so abruptly that water sloshed perilously close to the edge of the bath. The right reason for not throwing herself at him was because she would have looked an utter fool.

How many times did she have to remind herself that she and Tyler were headed in quite different directions? She wasn't part of his plan and she could hardly complain. He had been clear about that right from the start. *You're just not my type*, he had said. *Anyone except you.*

So, no more fantasies about kissing him, all right? No more dreams about touching him, feeling him, tasting him, letting her lips drift over the lean, muscled length of his body…

Mary swallowed and stood up, shaking that last thought aside. 'Idiot!' she chastised herself as she reached for a towel. Instead of keeping a careful guard over her emotions, she had let herself fall for that time out of time nonsense, and what was the result? She was halfway in love with Tyler Watts.

You would have thought that she would have known better. Her heart was still raw after the break-up with Alan. She should be cosseting it with some tender, loving care, not tossing it at the feet of a ruthless workaholic whose ambitions were fixed on a loveless marriage and a trophy wife. If she wasn't careful, her poor heart would get trampled all over again, and she would have no one to blame but herself. Tyler had made it very clear what he wanted right from the start, and it didn't include her.

She had to keep her heart safe from now on, Mary realised. For her own protection, she needed to remember just what she was doing here.

But it was hard when she went along to Bea's bedroom and found Tyler stretched out on the floor beside her daughter, patiently retrieving the toys she was throwing. He seemed to have done a very good job of cajoling her out of her bad mood, and she squealed happily and pointed when she saw her mother in the doorway.

Tyler turned his head quickly to see Mary in a skirt and the same soft top she had worn that first night, her hair still damp from the bath. She was smiling but there was a certain wariness in the lovely grey eyes, he thought.

'Better?' he asked, getting to his feet.

'Much, thank you. I feel like a new woman,' she

told him. 'Thanks for looking after Bea,' she went on. Bending to pick up her daughter gave her a good excuse to avoid his eyes. 'Come on, you,' she said with an 'ouf!' as she hoisted her up. 'I've had my time off. You'll need changing.'

But there was no tell-tale whiff from the nappy when she sniffed cautiously. Puzzled, Mary glanced at Tyler, who shrugged and looked awkward. 'I had a go,' he admitted.

'*You* changed her nappy?'

'You were in the bath,' he said almost defensively.

Mary's throat was so tight that she couldn't speak. Tyler had been so resolute in refusing to deal with nappies before that it had become something of a joke, but he had done it tonight, and her heart told her that he had done it for her.

'Thank you,' was all she could manage. Still holding Bea in her arms, she reached up and kissed him quickly on the cheek before she could change her mind.

His skin was rough beneath her lips and he smelt clean and masculine and, after the realisation that she would only have to turn her head a fraction to find his mouth, time seemed to freeze. Their bodies were very close. It was as if two magnets were being pulled irresistibly towards each other, and the yearning to press herself into him was enormous. Temptation yawned as Mary felt Tyler stiffen and his hands lift and for one thrilling moment she thought that he was going to pull her close. Dizzy with longing, she waited, until in the end he just let his arms fall back to his sides.

Only then, and much, much too late, did she remember her poor battered heart and make herself step away.

There was an awkward pause. Mary wanted to say something light, to pass the whole thing off as a joke, but there didn't seem to be enough oxygen to speak and the lack of it was making her breathless and giddy. It was as if the kiss had happened after all, and the air between them was twanging with what might have been.

For Mary it was as if she were standing on the edge of a cliff. It would be so easy to fall in love with him, so easy to succumb to temptation, to trust him with her heart and step out into light and space and glory. But what if she couldn't trust him? What if she fell and he didn't catch her and lift her up?

She couldn't risk it, Mary thought with the sudden panicky realisation of just how close she was to the edge. Perhaps she would have taken the chance if she only had herself to consider, but she had Bea to think about. She couldn't run the risk of falling apart if Tyler didn't love her back.

And he wouldn't. She knew that. No, Mary reminded herself, she had to be sensible. She had to remember the terms of their agreement, and the fact that she would be leaving soon.

She felt curiously detached. 'You know, now that you've changed a nappy, I'm not sure there's anything more I can teach you about how to have a successful relationship,' she said, meeting his eyes with careful composure. 'I think it's time you did something about putting all those lessons into practice. The month is nearly over.'

Tyler frowned. 'What do you mean?'

'Perhaps you should think about going out and meeting someone,' said Mary, turning casually away and rummaging in a drawer for a clean vest and top for Bea. 'There's not much point in us carrying on like this, is there?'

She had her back to him, and Tyler was glad that she couldn't see his face. He suspected he looked as if she had slapped him suddenly. That quick kiss had nearly undone him. Her lips had been soft, and he'd been able to smell the shampoo in her clean, damp hair. She'd been standing so close, he'd felt quite heady with it.

He had so nearly made a monumental fool of himself, Tyler realised. Without thinking, his arms had come up to pull her close, baby or no baby, and then where would they have been? His careful strategy of sticking to a friendly relationship would have looked a bit foolish then, wouldn't it? As it was, only a supreme effort of will had forced his arms back to his sides.

'No,' he said. 'No point at all.'

His head had still been reeling from her nearness when she had calmly reminded him of their professional arrangement. Tyler had been taken aback by the depth of his disappointment, but really, wasn't she suggesting what he himself wanted? It was easier this way. They were both going to be friendly but professional. It would be fine.

'I'll start dating again,' he promised, ignoring the hollow feeling deep inside him at the prospect. 'I'll meet someone soon.'

Perhaps inevitably, Mary inherited Bea's cold and her soaking the day before brewed it into a real humdinger. So now she had a thick head, red eyes and a streaming nose to add to her charms. Regarding her very unlovely reflection in the mirror that morning, Mary decided to stay at home.

She didn't have a car anyway, she remembered. There were buses, of course, but it would be a long walk to the nearest stop and there was no point in spreading her germs around. She might be committed to her agency, but there were limits.

Tyler rang her on her mobile at lunchtime. 'You're not answering your email,' he accused her. 'Where are you?'

'At home,' Mary croaked. 'I look disgusting and I feel worse.'

'Why didn't you let me know?' he demanded crossly.

'I thought I'd disrupted you enough at work yesterday,' she said through a fit of coughing. 'Anyway, there's nothing you can do. It's just a cold.'

Tyler grunted. 'Well, I'll be back early, anyway,' he said. 'I've got something for you.'

'All I need is a bottle of cough medicine and a barrel of paracetamol,' said Mary as best she could with her blocked nose.

'I'll bring that too,' said Tyler and rang off.

True to his word, he was back before five that evening. He found Mary on the sofa, within easy reach of a wastepaper basket overflowing with tissues, watching a chat show on television with a glazed expression.

'How do you feel?'

'Better than I look, actually,' she said, sitting up and pointing the remote control at the television to switch it off. She had had a whole day to realise that she had made the right decision yesterday. There was nothing to be gained from falling in love with Tyler, while being sensible, as she *was* being, would leave her with her heart, her pride and her bank balance intact. 'Did you bring any cough medicine, though?'

'I did. I brought something else too,' said Tyler. 'Do you think you could manage a quick trip outside?'

'Outside?'

Puzzled, Mary hauled herself to her feet, managing no less than four enormous sneezes in the process, and trying not to notice how trustingly Bea lifted her arms to him to be picked up. Her daughter would miss Tyler as much as she would when the time came to go.

Next week, Mary reminded herself sternly. Not some hypothetical, misty future. Her departure was only a matter of days away, and she had better get used to the notion.

'What is it?' she asked as Tyler opened the front door.

At the bottom of the steps sat a brand-new BMW. 'It's for you,' said Tyler.

'For me?' she said blankly.

'I had a word with the garage this morning. Your car's pretty much a write-off.'

Her face fell in dismay. There was no way she could afford another car at the moment. 'Oh, no.'

'So you can have this one,' Tyler went on. 'It's been insured in your name, and there's a car seat fitted for Bea.'

'That's a very expensive car to drive a baby around in,' said Mary, eyeing it doubtfully. 'Wouldn't it be better to hire something cheaper?'

'It's not hired,' he said haughtily. 'I bought it for you.'

Her jaw dropped. 'You're not serious!'

'Of course I'm serious,' said Tyler. 'Why wouldn't I be?'

'But that's…that's far too extravagant!' she protested. 'I'm only here for another ten days.'

His eyes flickered at the reminder, but then he shrugged carelessly. 'Keep it when you go.'

'I couldn't possibly accept an expensive car from you!'

'I thought you were short of money,' he said frowning.

'I am, but I'm not reduced to charity just yet,' said Mary touchily. 'I can hire a car for this week, and I won't need one so much when I'm back in town.'

Tyler made an exasperated noise. 'Why can't you just take this one? Think of it as a bonus, or part of your coaching fee.'

Mary shook her head firmly. 'Look, it's very generous of you, and I do appreciate the thought, but I can't take it. Quite apart from anything else, I could never afford to run it!'

He eyed her in frustration. 'We're supposed to be acting as if we had a real relationship,' he reminded her. 'If you were my girlfriend, there wouldn't be any problem about giving you a car.'

'Yes, but I'm not your girlfriend, am I?' said Mary a little tartly. 'And, even if I was, I wouldn't let you give me a car!'

'Why not? I thought women liked expensive presents—jewels and cars and trips to Paris and all that stuff.'

She sighed. 'I can't speak for all women, but personally, a present as expensive as that makes me uncomfortable. It just makes it obvious how unequal our incomes are. I don't want to feel that I'm being bought. A present is lovely if it's given in the right spirit as a romantic gesture.'

'What, like a diamond ring or something?'

'Exactly, but even then it doesn't have to be the biggest, showiest diamond around. I'd much rather have a ring that you'd chosen because you loved me—that *someone* had chosen because he loved me,' Mary corrected herself hastily. 'A thoughtful gesture means so much more than an ostentatious one.'

Ostentatious? Was that what she thought he was? Tyler scowled. 'I *am* being thoughtful,' he said crossly. 'I'm thinking that you're stuck out here in the country and you need transport to get to work.'

'Yes, but—' Mary bit her lip. 'I know you're being thoughtful,' she tried again, 'but saving me the trouble of hiring my own cheap little hatchback would have meant just as much, and not nearly as much as the fact that you changed Bea's nappy yesterday when I know you must have hated every minute of it!'

A muscle was jumping in Tyler's jaw. 'So you won't take the car?'

'No.'

He couldn't understand it. What was a miserable BMW to him? He couldn't imagine a single one of his previous girlfriends batting an eyelid about him giving them a car. Why did Mary have to be different? He'd imagined her screaming with excitement when she saw the car, had looked forward to watching her face as she sat behind the wheel and smelt the luxurious interior. He'd wanted her to be thrilled. Not for a minute had he thought that she would turn it down.

'At least use it while you're here,' he said grouchily, shutting the front door again with a bang.

Mary judged it time to give in gracefully. She could tell that she'd offended him, but honestly! What did he think she would do with a BMW? She didn't even have anywhere to live when she left here yet, and her mother's street was notorious as a route home from the city centre pubs. Cars were always having their wing mirrors snapped off, or being scraped by vans just too wide to squeeze through the narrow gap between the vehicles parked on either side of the road. A brand-new BMW wouldn't last a minute, and Mary didn't suppose they were cheap to repair. Tyler didn't seem to realise that not everyone had a garage or a stately home well away from passing yobs.

'All right, I'll do that,' she said. 'Thank you. I'll leave it here when I go next week. Who knows?' she said, trying to cajole him out of his bad mood. 'Maybe you'll meet someone perfect soon, and you can give her the car.'

'I hardly think my wife is the type to appreciate second-hand goods,' snapped Tyler.

More disappointed by her reaction than he

wanted to admit, he thrust Bea back to Mary. 'I'll be in my study,' he said, and stomped off.

Why couldn't she have been delighted with the car? Tyler thought morosely. Why couldn't she have jumped up and down and kissed him gratefully? Why couldn't she be slim and sweet and elegant?

Why couldn't she be the wife he wanted? He wanted a wife who would impress his peers, a woman so beautiful and stylish that every man would envy him. Who would envy him a plump, messy single mother?

It was just that whenever he tried to imagine his immaculate bride-to-be, her perfect face kept dissolving into a round one with big grey eyes, her smooth blond hair would be transformed into chaotic brown curls and her slender figure would swell until it was voluptuous and inviting.

She would turn into Mary, in fact—the same Mary who was going on and on and *on* about the fact that she was leaving soon. Anyone would think that she couldn't wait to go.

Supper that night was a tense meal, but Mary exerted herself to be chatty and as normal as possible, although it was hard when all she wanted was to kiss his bad humour away and coax him into a laugh.

Or she would have done if she wasn't being so resolutely sensible.

'Oh, I forgot to tell you,' she said as she sat down.

'I had a letter from Alan's solicitor today. It seems they're ready to agree to a valuation at long last. I don't know why they've suddenly got their act together, but at least it means that I should get my money soon.'

'That's good news,' said Tyler, who had already heard it from his own solicitors. He had charged them with putting a metaphorical boot up Alan's backside and it seemed they'd been effective.

'Isn't it?' Mary smiled brightly. 'I can think about finding somewhere to live now. I might have to rent at first, but that's all right. It means I can look around for a little house to buy without any pressure. In fact, I might go and register with some estate agents tomorrow,' she added, and produced another fixed smile. 'You'll have your house to yourself again in no time.'

That would teach him to be helpful, thought Tyler. He had only got in touch with his solicitors because he was outraged at the way Mary was being treated. He had thought a quiet intervention might be useful—showing that she had powerful friends prepared to flex a little muscle wouldn't go amiss.

Funny how he hadn't made the connection that helping Mary get her money would mean helping her to leave.

Still, it was just as well that she was thinking of moving out, he reasoned. It was bound to happen some time and better sooner than later. It would be easier to concentrate on his marriage strategy without her here, anyway.

'That's great,' he said, and then because it didn't sound that convincing first time round, he cleared his throat and said it again more forcefully. 'Great.'

In spite of this mutual insistence on the advantages of Mary moving out as soon as possible, it was not a particularly happy household. Far from being elated at having a seemingly intractable problem solved, Mary was tense, snappy and unaccountably depressed. Tyler was even worse. His normal irascibility seemed positively jolly compared to his mood over the next couple of days. Picking up on the strain in the atmosphere, Bea was fractious and grizzly.

Still, her cross little face dissolved into its usual beam when Tyler walked in that Friday evening, but his answering smile was cursory and he barely accorded her a pat on the head before he turned to Mary, tossing an embossed card on to the table between them.

'Carol reminded me about this today,' he said.

'What is it?'

'An invitation to a black tie reception in the Merchant Adventurers' Hall next Wednesday.'

Taking off his jacket, Tyler hung it over the back of a chair and loosened his tie. 'I need to go, and it looks better if I've got someone with me, so you'd better come along. I can practice being out with a partner, and who knows? I might meet someone new there and you can give me tips on how to make a good impression on her.'

Mary turned from the sink, wiping her hands on a tea towel. 'Do you want to try that again?' she asked with deceptive mildness.

'What do you mean?'

'Or shall we go over it step by step and work out all the ways you went wrong in one simple speech?'

Tyler had unbuttoned his cuffs and was rolling up his sleeves, and he glanced up from his task with undisguised irritation. 'I'm inviting you to a party, for God's sake!'

'Oh, that was an invitation, was it?' said Mary furiously. ' *"You'd better come along"*? My, you sure know how to sweep a girl off her feet, don't you?'

'Come on, Mary,' he said tetchily. 'We had a deal.'

'Yes, and the deal was that you treated me as you would a real girlfriend,' she said. 'And if you think any woman is going to be bowled over by having a card tossed towards her and informed that she'd better go along as you need someone with you, the implication being that you've got no one better to take, then you'd better think again! I might have other plans for next Wednesday.'

Tyler gave an exasperated snort. 'Have you?'

'As it happens, no,' she conceded, 'but you weren't to know that. And what were you thinking I would do with Bea? Just leave her here on her own?'

'Of course not. I assumed you'd be able to find a babysitter for her.'

'Don't *assume*,' said Mary, secretly relieved that she had a legitimate outlet for her bad temper over the last few days. *'Ask!'*

She hung up the tea towel and reached for a knife and a chopping board. 'Now, if you still want me to go to this reception, I suggest that you try that so-called invitation again—and I'd omit the part where you tell me that you're hoping to meet someone to replace me while I'm there, if I were you!'

'It's not about *replacing* you,' shouted Tyler, goaded. 'In case you've forgotten, you're not in fact my girlfriend!'

Mary's expression froze. 'There's no chance of me forgetting that, I can assure you,' she said icily—and quite untruthfully. She had been in serious danger of forgetting it until a few days ago.

'Well, then! I can't see what all the fuss is about!'

'You're still supposed to be practising your relationship skills, such as they are, on me,' said Mary in an acid voice. 'And that doesn't include treating me like the hired help, even if that's what I am.' She met his furious blue gaze squarely. 'So if you want me to go, ask me nicely.'

Tyler gritted his teeth. He had a good mind to go without her, but he needed her there. The logical part of his mind did ask why, given that he had attended plenty of functions on his own before, but she had made him so angry that he was beyond thinking rationally just then.

'Very well,' he said tightly. 'I'll start again. Are you doing anything next Wednesday, Mary?'

Mary put her head on one side as if flicking through a mental diary. 'I don't think so. Why?'

'I was wondering if you'd like to come to a reception at the Merchant Adventurers' Hall with me,' he ploughed on, only to break off as she held up a hand to stop him.

'Do you know, I think it would be a nice gesture if you told me how much you wanted me to go with you,' she suggested, sugar-sweet.

The muscle in Tyler's jaw was working overtime tonight. 'It would mean a lot to me if you came with me.'

'Hmm.' Mary considered. 'A bit stilted, but a vast improvement on your first attempt, anyway,' she pronounced.

Tyler stuck grimly to his role. 'Would you be able to find a babysitter for Bea?'

'I could ask my mother.'

'Can I take that as a yes?' After putting him through all that, she couldn't even be bothered to give him a straight answer!

Mary smiled graciously. 'If my mother's OK with looking after Bea, then yes, I'd love to come,' she said.

CHAPTER NINE

TEETERING a little on unfamiliar heels, Mary walked along the corridor to Tyler's office. She couldn't help remembering the heels she had worn the night of that reception, and how he had caught her as she fell. Sometimes she could swear her arm still tingled where he had gripped her.

It was hard to believe that had been only a month ago. Tyler had been a virtual stranger then, no more than her disagreeable ex-boss, and now…now he was part of her life. He was more than part of it, in fact. He was stuck smack in the middle of it, and in spite of all her strictures about staying sensible and protecting her heart, Mary was dismally aware of what a gaping hole he was going to leave in it when he had gone.

She had been doing her best to think positively about the future, and had even been to view a few flats, which turned out to be all that she was in a position to buy. Property was much cheaper than in London, of course, but nonetheless her options were still limited. Anything she could afford was going to seem very cramped after Haysby Hall. Luckily Bea was too small to notice or to miss the space.

Or Tyler.

Mary would, though. She was going to miss him terribly. She might have caught herself before she fell too deeply in love—she hoped—but it had been touch and go, and there was still a simmering physical attraction that she was doing her best to keep under control. But she was bearing up pretty well, she thought. Several stern conversations with herself had convinced her of the need to be sensible here. There was no chance of a future with Tyler, so one way or another she was just going to have to move on.

Moving on meant getting a grip on herself on more than just the emotional front. Mary had taken a good hard look at herself the night before and she hadn't liked what she saw. If she was going to have to go to this reception and watch while Tyler scanned the room for a prospective date, she wasn't going to look fat and frumpy while she was at it.

That morning she had blown half a month's rent on having her hair cut and coloured, and then she had bought the kind of dress that credit cards were invented for. There was no way that Mary could justify spending so much on a simple outfit but once she had made the mistake of trying it on, she had had to have it.

For such a tight-fitting dress it was surprisingly

flattering, clinging to all the right curves and falling in a lovely swish of heavy silk to disguise the wrong ones, and it had a daring neckline that managed to be sexy without being tarty.

Or so the girl in the shop had assured her. Looking down at the expanse of her cleavage on show, Mary wasn't so sure.

Still, it was too late to change now, and after spending all that money on the dress and matching shoes and a bag, because if you didn't have the right accessories you might as well not have bothered, she would just have to keep her chin up and pretend she didn't realise half her bosom was on show.

The building was eerily quiet at this time of night. Everyone had long gone and the offices were dimly lit, except in Tyler's office where a single reading light burned brightly.

Tyler was at his desk, frowning down at a draft contract, when Mary reached the open door and the breath dried in her throat at the sight of him. The lamp threw the severe lines of his face into sharp relief, and in his formal dinner jacket and bow-tie he looked dark and very formidable.

Intent on what he was reading, he hadn't heard her approach on the soft carpet. Mary smoothed her palms down the sides of her dress, swallowed and knocked lightly on the door.

Tyler looked up, briefly at first, and then he stared, the contract forgotten in his hand.

'Ready?' she asked.

'You've…you…you look different,' he said, so taken aback by the transformation in her that he could hardly get the words out.

'I've had my hair cut. What do you think?' She gave a self-conscious twirl.

Tyler couldn't think. She looked incredibly sexy in that dress that was clinging to all the right places, and proving that everything he had been imagining when he had seen her in her baggy layers or those shapeless pyjamas was all too true. He couldn't take his eyes off her.

And her hair… Tyler wasn't sure what the hairdresser had done, but she looked younger and more stylish, almost glamorous.

Almost beautiful.

His chest was so tight that he could hardly breathe. Belatedly, he dropped the contract on to the desk and pushed back his chair.

'You look…very…nice,' he said inadequately as he got to his feet.

Mary's brows rose slightly and he remembered one of their lessons. 'No, that's not right, is it?' he said. What was it she had told him once? *No woman ever wants to hear that she looks 'fine'.* 'If you were my girlfriend I would have to do better than that.'

'Indeed you would,' said Mary, glad to find that she had a voice after all. There had been a moment there as Tyler sat and simply stared when all the air had been sucked out of the room and she had wondered if she would ever breathe again. And now look at her! Not only could she string a few words together, she could even sound quite brisk and unperturbed while she was at it. Which was amazing, really, when you considered that her nerves were fluttering frantically beneath her skin and her pulse was booming in her ears.

'Your girlfriend will want to feel that the effort she's made is appreciated,' she went on, in the same cool voice that seemed to belong to someone else entirely. 'You should make her feel loved and desired.'

'As if I can't keep my hands off her?'

'Exactly.'

'As if I can't wait to take her home and make love to her? That I need her right here, right now?'

Mary lost her breath for a moment. 'That kind of thing, yes,' she said, retrieving it on a gasp.

'I see.' Tyler came round the desk towards her and took both Mary's hands in his, holding her still in his warm clasp so that he could study her face with those penetrating blue eyes. Mary was sure that he could see deep inside her, that he could tell that her entire body was thrumming with awareness, that he could hear the slow, painful thud of her heart.

His gaze dropped at last, but only to follow the curves of her body, and he inspected her all the way down to her peep-toe shoes in a silence that seemed to wrap itself around them until there were only the two of them in the whole world.

'There's only one word to describe you,' he said at last, and his voice was so deep that Mary felt it reverberate at the base of her spine.

She managed a nervous laugh. 'Fat?' she suggested, but Tyler shook his head.

'Gorgeous,' he said. 'You look absolutely gorgeous.'

Ridiculously, Mary blushed. 'Thank you,' she muttered.

'And if you were my girlfriend, I'd probably kiss you now, wouldn't I?' he went on. 'Just to prove how incredible I think you look.'

'You might do,' she agreed, her voice all over the place, 'but since I'm *not* in—'

'Why don't we pretend that you are?' Tyler interrupted her, his voice as deep and dark as treacle. 'After all, we might as well see the lesson through, and make sure I get it right next time.'

The trouble was, he realised later, that he wasn't thinking clearly. Somewhere at the back of his mind was the idea that he would give her a brief kiss to show Mary how great she looked. It would be a courtesy, no more than that, but that got lost the moment his eyes dropped to her mouth, so lush and inviting, and he forgot everything else but the need to possess it.

Bending his head, he captured her lips with his own, but the first touch of her mouth sent a great crashing wave of something that was far from mere politeness surging through him, and before he had thought properly what he was doing, he had yanked her in to him and was kissing her properly.

In his arms, he felt Mary stiffen for a moment, but the next her resistance had gone and she was melting into him, returning his kiss hungrily, almost angrily. It felt as if they were punishing each other, but at the same time it was out of their control, and there was nothing but taste and touch and feel and churning pleasure as the heat surged between them, searing, scorching and unstoppable.

Tyler's hands were hard on her, sliding demandingly down her back and pulling her closer, closer, and Mary clung to him, arching in to his body, gasping for breath between deep, deep kisses, heedless of anything but the wild, wicked pulse of need. He felt so strong, so solid, so *good*, and his lips were so sure.

She could feel herself dissolving in the sweet swirl of sensation, and the sense of losing herself was so powerful that she clutched harder, holding on to him as if he were the only fixed point in the universe, and when she felt him start to lift his head she murmured deep in her throat in protest, not wanting to face the moment when she had to let him go.

Tyler was so shaken by the loss of control that for

a long moment after he broke that long, long kiss he could only stare at her, his heart jerking madly as he struggled for breath. He couldn't believe what had happened, how utterly he had been carried away, intoxicated by her softness and her sweetness and her warmth.

Mary looked totally shocked, he realised, appalled. What had he done? Her grey eyes were dark and dilated, and no wonder. Tyler remembered kissing her once before and how dangerously seductive that had been, but it had been nothing like this.

It was the worst thing that he could have done. He didn't want to know that kissing Mary could be like that. She was leaving and their paths were diverging, and what was he going to say when she asked him why he had grabbed her like that? What *could* he say? God, how could he have been such a fool?

Losing control, being stupid, looking a fool… It was Tyler's nightmare scenario, and somehow Mary was the cause of it all, he thought, half baffled, half resentful. She had turned his life upside down, changing everything, making him behave in ways he couldn't explain, even to himself.

'I'm sorry,' he said raggedly at last, turning away from that great grey gaze and raking a hand through his hair. 'I got a bit carried away there. I wasn't thinking. I forgot it was you.'

Translation: I didn't mean to kiss you at all. I didn't *want* to kiss you.

With an enormous effort, Mary managed to pull herself together. Her body was still throbbing, every sense pulsating, and she wanted nothing more than to throw herself back into the arms of a man who had forgotten who she was, and who wouldn't have wanted her if he had remembered in time.

'Don't worry about it,' she said a little shakily. 'I'll take it as a compliment to my dress. And it's just the thing you ought to do when your real girl-friend turns up so, all in all, I'd give you full marks.'

There, that ought to show him that she hadn't taken that shattering kiss seriously, but her legs were trembling as she escaped to the Ladies, and her hand shook horribly as she tried to repair her lipstick.

Tyler had arranged for a driver to take them to the Merchant Adventurers' Hall, and Mary didn't know whether to be glad or sorry. On the plus side, she would have been struggling on her heels, even if her legs had been functioning normally. As it was, her bones seemed to have melted and were doing a re-markable impression of cotton wool. It was a miracle she managed to stay upright in the lift, let alone contemplate a trek across the river and through the cobbled streets.

So a lift meant that Tyler wouldn't have to abandon her halfway, crumpled in a boneless heap in some alleyway, and that was something. On the other hand, she was going to have to sit in a dark, enclosed space with him in the back of the car, and Mary wasn't sure if that might not be worse.

Once there, she decided that it was. She was desperately aware of Tyler next to her in the darkness. He was like a stranger, remote and forbidding, and he was very careful not to touch her, but the space between them vibrated with tension. Mary clutched her hands together in her lap and stared straight ahead, while every nerve in her body strained towards Tyler. She wanted to crawl over him, to kiss the grim set of his jaw until he smiled. She wanted to press her lips to the pulse in his throat, to feel his rough masculine skin and breathe in the scent of him.

It was a huge relief when they got to the Merchant Adventurers' Hall and she could put some distance between them. Mary practically fell out of the car in her haste and when Tyler made to take her by the elbow as they walked through the narrow stone gateway and across the courtyard she stepped quickly out of reach.

'We don't want to look as if we're together,' she said without looking at him.

'I thought that was the whole point,' said Tyler, exasperated. He was in a foul mood, and having to keep his hands off Mary in the back of the car hadn't improved matters. 'I'm supposed to be practising on you.'

'I thought you were finding someone to date?'

He hesitated, confused now about what the hell he was doing there at all. 'That, too.'

'You don't want me hanging on your arm if you're trying to chat somebody up, do you?' Mary pointed out. 'That would just cramp your style.'

What style? Tyler wondered as they made their way into the medieval hall with its spectacular timber roof. He scowled. He loathed occasions like this, as Mary knew perfectly well. It had obviously slipped her mind that he was paying her to be here. Instead of supporting him discreetly, she took the first opportunity to leave his side and was soon chatting animatedly at the other end of the hall.

There was a whole group around her, mostly men, Tyler noted grimly, watching her through the crowd, and he couldn't really blame them. She looked fantastic tonight, warm and sexy and alive, her face alight with intelligence and humour. It wasn't her fault that he wished she would go back to being the dowdy, mumsy figure she had been a month ago.

He didn't like the way those men were looking at her. He liked being the only one who noticed how warm and soft she was. Now everybody knew and everybody wanted to talk to her and she couldn't spare him so much as a glance.

Morosely, Tyler accepted a drink and reminded himself of his objective. There must be loads of women here. Surely he could find one who would like to go out? But he was soon buttonholed by men in suits who wanted to talk business to him, while over their shoulders he could see Mary laughing and flirting and apparently having a good time. She seemed to have forgotten that she came here with him, he thought jealously.

But no, here she came, tucking her hand into his elbow, smiling charmingly at his companions. 'Would you excuse Tyler a moment?' she said to them. 'There's someone I want him to meet.'

How come he could never extricate himself from situations like that? He was either stuck or had to go for the brutally rude option and simply walk away. Feeling inadequate, Tyler glowered.

'For God's sake, lighten up,' said Mary out of the corner of her mouth. 'No one's going to want to go out with you looking like that! Remember what I told you about smiling.'

But Tyler didn't feel like smiling. He glanced at Mary, determinedly tugging him across the room. Obviously that kiss hadn't meant anything to her, because she hadn't lost sight of the business in hand. And he shouldn't either, he thought glumly.

'Who am I meeting?'

'Her name's Fiona. I think you'll like her. She's very pretty, very stylish—blond, of course—and intelligent too. She's something in insurance, I'm not sure what. Perfect for you, anyway,' said Mary briskly. 'I thought she was rather nice, *and* she told me that she's recently split up with a long-term boy-friend. I reckon she's in her late twenties, so probably ready to think about settling down and having children soon.'

'Who turned you into my pimp?' Tyler demanded grouchily. 'You're supposed to be advising me on relationship matters, not trawling for prospective partners.'

Mary stopped and faced him in exasperation. 'You're the one who said you wanted to start dating again!'

'I do, but I can find my own girlfriend, thank you.'

'You won't find one talking business with a load of middle-aged men,' she pointed out. 'You've got to circulate. You haven't moved for half an hour. What were you talking about that was so fascinating?'

'The exchange rate,' Tyler admitted.

'Boy, you really are in the right frame of mind for romance, aren't you?'

'No,' he said. 'So we might as well not waste any more time here.'

He made to turn to the door, but Mary pulled him back. 'At least come and meet Fiona,' she said. 'I've told her about you and you might as well since you're here.'

So Tyler let himself be dragged over and intro-duced to Fiona, who was, annoyingly, everything

Mary had said she would be. Mary stood chatting with them for a while before she excused herself unobtrusively and left them to it.

She seemed very anxious to fob him off on someone else, Tyler thought crossly. It was all very well introducing him to someone else, but how could he concentrate on what Fiona was saying when she was standing only a few feet away letting some man practically fall down the front of her dress?

Turning his back, Tyler did his best to make conversation with Fiona, but he was acutely aware of Mary, and every now and then he would hear her laugh above the hubbub.

Fiona didn't draw attention to herself like that. She was much more discreet. As Mary had said, she was very pleasant. Tyler made himself focus on her advantages. She was intelligent, elegant, *classy*…just what he was looking for, in fact, he reminded himself. She was wearing a perfect little black dress, not a scene-stealer with a plunging neckline that had all the men cross-eyed. She wasn't laughing too loud or flirting or drinking too much champagne.

Mary was doing all three.

Mary wasn't classy. She wasn't beautiful. She wasn't elegant. She wasn't even blond. She was the last kind of woman he'd want for a wife. He was very glad she was planning to move out soon. Only a few more days and he would have his life back, and what a relief that would be.

Tyler made laboured conversation with Fiona for as long as he could, and they exchanged business cards. As Fiona handed hers to him, he was assailed by the memory of Mary giving him her card a month ago. Dammit, did everything have to remind him of her?

What was it going to be like when she was gone?

Empty, a voice inside him answered immediately. Lonely. Desolate.

Tyler pushed the voice aside. What rubbish. He had managed perfectly well without Mary Thomas for forty-three years. He hadn't been lonely before and there was no reason why he should start now His life had been a lot easier and more under control, and he had got a lot more work done. Everything would go back to normal. Except he'd have someone like Fiona living with him instead of Mary.

Tyler wasn't any good at circulating. He couldn't ease himself in and out of groups the way Mary seemed to be able to do. He bumped into his Financial Director though, so they talked work for a while, and then somebody buttonholed him about city parking charges, and all the while he was aware of Mary, smiling and chatting to everyone except him.

At length he could stand it no longer. Muttering a brusque excuse, he went over and took her by the arm. 'I think it's time we went,' he said pulling her away from a very disappointed-looking man in mid-conversation.

Mary was furious. 'I was talking to him!' she said, shaking her arm free.

'Talking?' snarled Tyler. 'Is that what they call it nowadays?'

'Oh, for heaven's sake! You can't just drag someone away from a conversation.'

'You did when I was talking earlier,' he pointed out, and she rounded on him.

'*I* was polite and acknowledged the other people and apologised and made an excuse! You just grabbed. I didn't even have time to give him my card. He's got a small business and I could have had some work from him, which is lost now, thanks to you!'

'You're supposed to be working for me,' said Tyler grimly.

The grey eyes flashed with temper. 'I am working for you, but you're not my only client,' she pointed out in an icy voice. 'I've got a business to run, and I need to make contacts. As it happens, it's been a very useful evening—or it was until you interfered!—and I picked up a lot of potential clients.'

'I'm not surprised, wearing that dress!' he said unpleasantly. 'I just hope you're prepared for exactly what kind of contact all those "potential clients" are interested in!'

'At least none of them will have to blackmail me into a job!' Mary snapped back. 'It's a nice change talking business with people who are happy to keep things on a professional level.'

'Oh, so you're not going to insist on moving in with everyone who offers you a recruitment contract then?'

Mary's eyes narrowed at his snide look. 'No, I won't be making that mistake again,' she said point-edly. 'As a matter of fact, I met a nice estate agent tonight who says he's got some great properties to show me. I'm going to have a look tomorrow.'

'Well, I'm sorry to break up your successful evening schmoozing,' said Tyler, scowling at the thought of Mary looking at places to live, 'but it's half past ten. I thought you'd be anxious to go and make sure that your daughter was all right.'

'She'll be fine with Mum,' huffed Mary, but in truth she wasn't that sorry to have to leave.

It had been an exhausting evening. Sparkling and being vivacious was hard work when you had been kissed to shattering effect by a man who hadn't meant to kiss you at all, and when you had to spend the rest of the evening trying to convince him that you hadn't taken it seriously. Mary was tired and tense, unable to decide what she wanted most, to thump Tyler, to throw herself into his arms, or to burst into tears.

Stalking off wasn't an option either. They still had to pick up Bea, and then the chauffeur was driving them back to Haysby Hall. Mary was dreading the journey, alone in the dark with Tyler. The only way to get through it was to stay bolshy. If she reminded herself enough of how difficult and disagreeable he was being tonight, there would be less temptation to slide over the back seat towards him.

'So,' she said brightly as they waited on the pavement for the car to appear. 'How did you get on with Fiona?'

'Fine,' he said tersely.

'Didn't you think she was pretty?'

'She's very attractive, yes.'

'Did you ask her out?'

'I said I'd give her a call,' said Tyler, resenting this interrogation.

'Well, you'd better try harder to make a better impression on the phone than you did tonight,' said Mary frankly.

He glared at her. 'What do you mean? What was I doing wrong?'

'Let's see,' she said, casting her eyes upwards in a parody of deep thought. 'You were in a foul mood, you were remote and unfriendly, you didn't seem the slightest bit interested in her... Shall I go on?'

'I *was* interested in her,' Tyler insisted, not entirely truthfully. 'I said I'd call her, didn't I?'

'I bet she won't be expecting you to get in touch,' said Mary, turning down her mouth. 'You weren't giving out any of the right signals.'

'Rubbish!'

'I'm serious. I didn't see you smile once! If you'd wanted her to think that you were really interested, you should have been asking her questions, making eye contact, mirroring her body language, even touching her very lightly. You just stood there and looked grim.'

'It worked, didn't it?' said Tyler, annoyed. 'She gave me her card.'

'It's a big step from getting a business card to getting married,' Mary pointed out as the car purred to a halt beside them at last. 'You're going to have to make a lot more effort next time you see her— and you've got to persuade her to go out with you first! If I were Fiona, I'd be hanging out for someone a lot more fun!'

Of course, the trouble was that she *wasn't* Fiona, and she didn't want anyone more fun. The truth was that she wanted Tyler, and no one else would do.

But she couldn't have him, largely *because* she wasn't Fiona, so she was just going to have to get over it, Mary told herself. Still, she couldn't help secretly hoping that Fiona would refuse Tyler's invitation.

Sadly, Fiona didn't refuse. Tyler came home from work the next day and reported that he would be taking her out to dinner on Friday night. Stung by Mary's comments, he had rung Fiona that morning. He was annoyed to find that, just as Mary had predicted, Fiona was surprised to hear from him, but he was able to tell Mary that she had sounded delighted by his invitation.

'That's good,' said Mary, busy at the hob and glad of the excuse not to face him. 'You won't be needing any supper tomorrow night, then.'

That was it, concentrate on the practicalities. It was easier that way.

'No.' Tyler bent down to Bea, who was holding her arms up to him imperatively and demanding his attention in no uncertain terms.

Her little body was warm and solid as he picked her up, and her face was wreathed in smiles the instant she had got her own way. She beamed at him and bumped her head against his in an attempt at a kiss, and Tyler's heart twisted painfully at the realisation that he wouldn't be here to pick her up tomorrow night. He wouldn't be coming home to a warm kitchen and a smiley baby and to Mary.

Joggling Bea in his arms, Tyler glanced at her mother. At least Mary wasn't wearing that dress tonight, which was a lot easier on his blood pressure. Instead she had on loose trousers and some kind of fine-knit cardigan, neither of which were in the least sexy or provocative, but with her new haircut she looked unusually stylish.

Tyler wished she would go back to her baggy layers. He wished that she would turn round and smile at him. He wished he wasn't taking Fiona out to dinner tomorrow night.

Quite suddenly, Tyler felt cold and rather sick. He was making the most terrible mistake, he realised.

'Mary—' he began urgently, but she had turned at last and had started speaking at exactly the same time.

They both stopped and there was an awkward pause. 'You first,' said Tyler, who hadn't really known what he was going to say anyway.

'I was just going to say that I saw a great flat today,' she said a little stiltedly. 'It's perfect for us.'

'Us?' he echoed without thinking, and she looked at him strangely.

'Bea and I,' she explained.

'Oh. Yes.' Of *course* just Bea and her, you fool! Tyler burned with humiliation. You didn't think she meant to include you, did you?

Mary had reminded him of the reality of the situation just in time. She was leaving anyway. There was no point in blurting out that he had changed his mind like some big kid, or telling her that he would rather stay in with her and Bea than go out with Fiona. She would just raise those odd brows of hers, remind him that he was paying her a lot of money to get to this point, and make him feel like an idiot.

Tyler didn't like feeling stupid.

'Are you going to take it?' he asked.

'I think so.' Mary dipped her wooden spoon in the sauce she was making and tasted it cautiously. 'It's a good price, but the current tenant's still there. I wouldn't be able to move in for another couple of weeks.'

'You can stay here until then, if you want,' said

Tyler, ultra-casual, but inwardly aghast at how much wanted her to agree. 'It would suit me. After all, now I'm dating, this is when I'm going to need your advice most.'

Mary stirred her sauce, not meeting his eyes. 'I'll think about it,' she said.

She was giving Bea her breakfast when Tyler appeared on Saturday morning. He was normally long gone before she got downstairs, even at weekends, but perhaps he made an exception after a heavy date, she thought drearily.

'Hi.' She managed to greet him casually enough, even though her heart had given a sickening lurch at the sight of him. 'There's coffee in the pot if you want it. It should still be hot.'

'Thanks.'

Tyler might be uncharacteristically late down to breakfast, but otherwise he was as taciturn as usual. He went over to pour himself some coffee, and Mary watched his back with a kind of resentment. He was arrogant, impatient and grumpy and he had spent the whole of yesterday evening romancing another woman. It wasn't fair that he could still melt her bones just by standing there.

Yesterday had been the longest evening Mary had ever known. Even when things had been at their worst with Alan, she hadn't felt this dreary and hopeless. She had eaten a lonely supper and looked in vain for something to watch on television, but when she had tossed the remote away in disgust and had gone to have a bath, not even the determined listing of all the great things about the new flat could distract her mind for long from the fact that Tyler was out with Fiona.

Fiona would be sitting across the table from him in some intimately lit restaurant. It was Fiona whose eyes would settle on his mouth, Fiona who would see the way his cool eyes warmed and the crease deepened in his cheek when he smiled. Fiona, whose hands Tyler might reach across the table to hold, Fiona who would wonder what it would be like to kiss him.

Mary could have told her. Mary had tortured herself by imagining what Tyler was doing, what he was thinking. Would he just say goodbye at the end of the date, or would he kiss Fiona? If he thought she was right for him, he wouldn't waste any time pussyfooting around. Mary knew him too well to believe that.

No, Tyler had set out very clear specifications for the wife he wanted, and Fiona fitted them perfectly. She was the kind of woman any man would be proud to have on his arm. Tyler might not have seemed very enthusiastic when he first met her, but Mary knew how completely he focused on his goal. With terrier-like persistence, he wouldn't change his mind once it was made up, and he wouldn't give up until he had got exactly what he wanted.

And that wasn't her. She had known that a long time, but it wasn't getting any easier to accept. It had become plain to Mary that long, dismal evening that she couldn't stay here. She might understand why Tyler wanted to date other women, but that didn't mean she had to like it, and she didn't have to bear it if she didn't want to. The more his relationship with Fiona developed, the harder it was going to get. Better to go now, Mary had decided.

'More coffee?' Tyler asked, lifting the pot enquiringly in Mary's direction.

'Thank you.' She pushed her mug across the table towards him and took a breath. 'So,' she said brightly, 'how was your date last night?'

'Fine,' said Tyler. His favourite adjective.

'Is that all? Fine?'

'No, it was more than fine,' he said, but it hadn't felt fine. It had felt all wrong to be out with Fiona when Mary was at home, putting Bea to bed, cooking in the warm kitchen.

And then *that* had felt all wrong. After all, Tyler had told himself, he was sitting in the best restaurant in York with a beautiful woman who was interested, friendly, intelligent and everything he could possibly want in a bride. He ought to be pleased with himself, not wishing that he was sitting in the kitchen with a baby on his lap, his tie loosened, having his nose pulled by inquisitive fingers, and watching Mary move around, the intent expression on her face as she tasted a sauce, her smile as she lifted Bea out of the high chair, the way she rolled her eyes if he said something she disagreed with.

Fiona didn't disagree with him. She didn't point out his faults or make him take back something he'd said. She wasn't astringent, and she didn't make him cross, but she didn't make him laugh either. She didn't knock over her wine.

She wasn't Mary.

But she *was* what he was looking for, Tyler had reminded himself doggedly as the evening dragged past. Mary wasn't what he wanted.

He wasn't what Mary wanted either, judging by the businesslike cross-examination he was getting about his date.

'Well, go on,' she said. 'You've got to tell me a bit more than that. What was she wearing?'

Tyler searched his memory, which was unhelpfully blank. 'A dress, I think.'

So informative. Mary rolled her eyes. 'Did she look nice?'

'Yes.' He was sure about that at least.

'Did you tell her that?'

'I can't remember,' he said irritably. 'What does it matter?'

'It matters if you wanted it to be a successful date and wanted her to look forward to another one,' said Mary. 'You should have been making an effort to make *her* feel as if you were really pleased and proud to be out with her. She won't be telepathic. She won't know you like her unless you give her all those little signals I told you about—touching her lightly, making eye contact, being really open with each other. Did you do *any* of that?'

'She agreed to come out to dinner again next week,' Tyler said, aware that he was sounding on the defensive, and avoiding the question. 'So I can't have got it that wrong.'

'I hope you're going to call her today and say that you enjoyed your evening and that you're looking forward to seeing her again?'

'Look, Fiona's a sensible woman. She won't expect me to jump through those kind of hoops.'

'Showing that you appreciate someone and have been thinking about them isn't a *hoop*,' said Mary, exasperated. 'Haven't I taught you anything?'

'Why do you care?' Tyler demanded abrasively.

'It's my job to care,' she reminded him. 'And I want my second five thousand pounds,' she added, cucumber cool. 'We agreed I wouldn't get that until you were settled in a relationship, and one date hardly counts as one of those, does it?'

'Oh, yes, your money,' he said, tossing back his coffee and getting to his feet. 'We don't want to forget what you're doing here, do we? I shouldn't worry, though. It looks as if you'll be getting your extra five thousand. I think Fiona's going to be perfect.'

CHAPTER TEN

THERE was a tiny pause.

'So…that's good news for both of us, then, isn't it?' said Mary.

'Very good,' Tyler agreed. 'Well, I'm off,' he went on after a moment's silence while they both reflected on just how good the news felt.

Or not.

'Where are you going?'

'To the office. I've got some reports to read.' He could have brought them home to read at the weekend, but there was no use pretending that he would be able to concentrate. Besides, he couldn't hang around Mary and Bea all day and he couldn't think of anything else he wanted to do.

Mary was biting her lip. 'I didn't realise you would be going out this morning,' she said. 'I'd better say goodbye now then.'

'I'll be back later,' said Tyler, checking that he had his wallet.

'I won't be here,' said Mary. 'Bill's coming to pick us up this morning.'

'Pick you up?' He looked up sharply. 'What for?'

'I'm moving out.'

Tyler felt as if he'd been kicked in the stomach. 'I didn't think your flat was going to be ready for a couple of weeks.' He'd been *counting* on it not being ready. For some reason he didn't feel able to face right then.

'We can stay with Mum and Bill until then.'

'What's wrong with here?'

How could she tell him that she couldn't bear seeing him and Fiona together?

'I…just think it would be better if I go now,' she said carefully, not meeting his eye. 'After all, my work here is done,' she added, trying to make a joke of it. 'You've started a relationship with Fiona. I know it's only at the very early stages, but you'll do better without me around all the time. What if you want to bring her back here? It wouldn't be very romantic if she found your relationship coach making cocoa in the kitchen!'

Tyler frowned. He couldn't imagine Fiona here. This was Mary's kitchen. 'We're nowhere near that stage yet.'

'Well, you never know… Anyway, I'm ready to move out.' She mustered a bright smile. 'It's been great being here and giving Mum and Bill some space for a while, but it'll be good to get back to town. This is a lovely house, but it's not exactly convenient, is it?'

That was it, focus on the disadvantages and not on how much she was going to miss the space and the quiet and the beautiful kitchen and having Tyler come home every night.

His expression hardened. 'If you want to move out, I suppose there's nothing I can do to stop you,' he said curtly. 'I trust you'll remember that we still have an agreement, though? Two months, you said.'

'I haven't forgotten,' said Mary with dignity. 'Naturally, I'll be available for feedback and advice if you need it.'

Feedback! Tyler was furious, and not even sure why. 'I'd better make sure you have a cheque now then, as the first instalment of your account,' he said.

'There's no need to do it straight away,' she said uncomfortably.

But Tyler was already striding off to his study. Scrawling out a cheque, he ripped it out of the book so savagely that it tore and he had to write a fresh one, which did nothing to improve his temper.

'There you are,' he said, dropping it on to the table. 'The first instalment of your fee.'

So it had come to this. Mary felt sick. 'Tyler—'

'I'll be in touch before my next date with Fiona,' he overrode her. 'You can help me prepare for that.'

What could she say? 'You know where to find me,' she said quietly.

Tyler hesitated, his anger draining out of him suddenly. 'Well…goodbye, then,' he said.

Mary tried a smile, but it wavered so much that she had to compress her mouth into a straight line. 'Goodbye,' she managed.

There was a horrible silence while they just looked at each other, and then Tyler roused himself and headed for the door. He hadn't made it before an outraged squeal from Bea made him turn instinctively. She had never taken kindly to being ignored and was bouncing indignantly up and down in her high chair, chubby arms stretched out towards him.

How could he walk away from her? Setting his jaw, Tyler went back.

Bea beamed with pleasure and demanded to be picked up. Unable to resist the iron will of an infant, he lifted her and held her close for a moment, careless for once of her smeary mouth or her sticky hands on his shirt. As she cuddled happily in to him, Tyler breathed in her clean baby smell and closed his eyes against the crack of his heart.

He kissed the soft, fine hair once. 'Bye, Bea,' he said, and his throat was so tight that it was hard to get the words out.

Passing her to Mary was one of the hardest things he had ever done. 'She'll miss you,' said Mary, the luminous grey eyes shimmering with tears.

Tyler didn't trust himself to speak. He nodded abruptly and turned on his heel.

That wasn't what Bea wanted at all. Her face puckered and she started to cry, straining after him so desperately that Mary had to struggle to hold her.

Her wails followed Tyler down the corridor. He slammed the front door against them, but they were still ringing in his ears as he got into the car, and he dropped his head on to the steering wheel, squeezing his eyes shut for a long moment. Then he straightened, took a deep breath and switched on the ignition, and he drove away along the long avenue without looking back.

It was nearly dark before Tyler came home that night. The beam of his headlights lit up the BMW parked under the spreading cedar, and his heart leapt. Mary was still here!

But as soon as he opened the front door, the emptiness of the house settled around him like a stone. There was a note on the kitchen table.

Thank you for everything. I'm leaving the car, but we've taken out the baby seat. Fiona didn't seem like the kind of girl who would object to a car that's only been used for a week, so perhaps it will find another grateful driver. Let me know when you're ready for more coaching. I'm always available for consulta-

tion—or to help with any recruitment problems you may have! Good luck with Fiona.
Love, Mary.
PS Casserole in fridge. Have rung Mrs Palmer and she'll start cooking for you again next week.

Love, Mary? Tyler crumpled the note in one fist and swore as he threw it at the wall. *Love*, Mary! She didn't love him. If she'd loved him she wouldn't have left him alone in this great, empty house with a *casserole* to console him!

The kitchen felt desolate without them. Tyler looked around him, as if unable to believe that the high chair had gone, and Bea with it. She wasn't there, banging her spoon on the tray and shouting for attention. Mary wasn't at the hob, wrapped in Mrs Palmer's apron. There was only the empty room and the background buzz of the fridge to emphasise the silence.

Setting his jaw, Tyler went over to the fridge and took out the casserole. He wasn't hungry, but he wasn't about to go into a decline. He had faced worse times than this, and he had learnt that the only way to get through them was to keep his head down and plough on. Giving up wasn't in his vocabulary. There was no point in sitting around moping. He would just have to get on with it. It was high time he got back to work anyway.

But, as he sat at his desk, he found himself listening for the sound of Mary's footsteps upstairs, of Bea protesting at having her nappy changed. The house echoed with their absence. Tyler stared unseeingly down at the budget he was supposed to be reading and for the first time in years remembered how he had felt as a little boy when his mother had died.

He threw the papers down and pushed back his chair. God, he'd be crying next! It was time to pull himself together.

Defiantly, he pulled out Fiona's card and dialled the number to ask her out for a drink the next evening. See, he was getting on with his life already. He would be back to normal in no time.

He woke on Sunday morning with a sick feeling in the pit of his stomach that he dismissed as a bug of some kind. He would ignore it the way he ignored every other bug and eventually it would go away. The day stretched interminably. When Mary and Bea were around there never seemed to be enough time, but now it yawned joylessly before him, day after day without them.

His date with Fiona that evening was all that kept him going, reassuring him that he was sticking to his strategy, but the drink was not a huge success. Tyler made an effort to remember everything Mary had told him, but he hadn't counted on the fact that every time he tried to put some of her advice into practice, he would end up thinking about her instead of Fiona. *Make eye contact*, Mary had said, but whenever he met Fiona's beautiful blue gaze he would hear Mary's crisp voice and the blueness blurred before the memory of grey eyes that danced with teasing laughter.

Still, he persevered, because giving up wasn't an option. It was a relief to say good night and go their separate ways at the end of the evening, but that didn't stop Tyler asking Fiona out to dinner the following weekend. He wasn't prepared to admit that the invitation had given him the perfect excuse to contact Mary, but it probably *would* be a good idea.

After all, he was paying her for her advice, Tyler reasoned, and he was quite used to her being gone. He was back in his old routine. It was nonsense to think that he might still miss Mary and Bea. That kind of thing was just sentimental twaddle. His goal hadn't changed, and nor had his strategy.

He waited until Wednesday—any earlier would look as if he couldn't wait to see her again—and surprised Carol by telling her that he would be taking a lunch break. He didn't want to make an appointment. He would just turn up at Mary's office and have a chat with her, maybe take Bea out for a walk. It didn't need to be a formal meeting, did it? He just needed to see her.

For coaching, Tyler added hastily to himself.

Feeling ridiculously nervous, he climbed the rickety stairs and knocked on the door.

'Come in!'

Tyler took a breath and opened the door. Mary was sitting behind her desk and she looked up with a smile that froze at the sight of him.

For a long, long moment they just stared at each other, then Mary got numbly to her feet and came round the desk.

'Hello.' Her voice was thready with shock. She had dreamt of this, without ever letting herself believe that it could happen.

The last few days had been wretched. Leaving Tyler might have been the sensible thing to do, but she hadn't realised that missing him would hurt so much. Time and again, she had picked up the phone to ring him, just needing to hear his voice, before she made herself put it down again.

Be sensible, her head would remind her firmly, while her heart cracked with the need to see him again, to be near him. And now there he was, standing in the doorway, and Mary was almost afraid to move in case he turned into a chimera that she had conjured up with the power of her longing, and that would vanish cruelly if she got too close.

'Are you busy?' Tyler asked stiltedly.

'I've got an appointment at two o'clock, but I've got a few minutes now,' she said, hardly able to believe that she could carry on an apparently normal conversation. She swallowed. 'Come in.'

She gestured Tyler towards the easy chairs and took one herself. They sat facing each other as the silence lengthened uncomfortably.

Mary tried desperately to get a grip, but she felt suddenly overwhelmed. It was like being in a tumble-dryer of emotion at the moment, missing Tyler, longing to see him, dreading seeing him, and now the sheer joy of simply being near him again, on top of Alan's unexpected phone call, which had thrown everything into question once more.

She couldn't look at Tyler properly. She was afraid that she might do something stupid, like blurting out how much she had missed him or how good it was to see him again, so instead of meeting his gaze calmly like a professional meeting one of her clients, her eyes skittered nervously over his face and away in panic whenever they met his pale blue ones.

Tyler broke the awkward silence. 'You're looking good,' he said.

She was, too. It had taken him a little while to get used to it, but her hair really suited her like that, and she was wearing a scoop-necked top with a long skirt and boots that made her look businesslike but approachable.

'Thanks.' Mary smiled briefly. 'How are you?'

'Fine, fine.' He looked around the office, not

wanting to think about how he was without her. 'Where's Bea?'

'She's with my mother today. I had several interviews arranged, so I thought it would be easier without her.'

Tyler wanted to ask Mary if Bea missed him, if *she* missed him, but he didn't know how to without looking pathetic.

There was another agonising pause.

'Well,' said Mary at last. 'What can I do for you?'

Time to get down to business, obviously. 'I'm having dinner with Fiona this Saturday,' he said. 'I wondered if you'd have time for a bit of…preparation.'

'Now?'

Tyler felt like a fool. 'Unless you'd prefer a drink tonight?' Funny how he had never felt the slightest bit awkward until he met Mary, and now he seemed to be blundering around getting everything wrong all the time.

'I can't tonight.' She bit her lip. 'Alan's coming up from London.'

'*Alan?*' He stared at her, his heart sinking. 'Bea's father?'

'Yes.' Mary swallowed. 'He rang a couple of days ago. He's been thinking about Bea, he says. He wants us to get back together.'

There had been months when Mary would have given everything she possessed to hear Alan telling her that. It was ironic that he should ring when she had realised just how much she loved another man.

A lead weight was settling heavily inside Tyler. He hadn't been expecting this. He had thought that Mary might be distant, preoccupied with work or her new flat, but he had never imagined that Alan would reappear. He remembered her face when she had told him how desperately she had loved Bea's father.

'What are you going to say?' he heard himself ask.

'I…don't know,' said Mary truthfully. 'I have to consider it at least. He's Bea's father.'

'He hasn't been much of a father so far.'

'No, but he's the only father she has. If there's a chance of her growing up with two parents, I can't dismiss it out of hand. It's not as if Alan and I didn't love each other. We could love each other again.'

'Sure he hasn't just decided that it would be cheaper to take you back than pay you the money he owes you?' asked Tyler snidely, and then regretted it when he saw her face change. 'Sorry,' he said. 'That was uncalled for.'

Mary dropped her head into her hands and rubbed her temples wearily. 'I just don't know what to do,' she admitted. 'I suppose part of me is hoping that the old magic will come back when I see him, but it's been such a long time, I don't know what it will be like. All I know is that I have to do what's best for Bea.'

'I see,' said Tyler.

'Anyway,' said Mary, lifting her head, 'that's my problem. I shouldn't be bothering you with it.' She summoned a smile. 'I'm the one who's supposed to be the relationship expert around here, after all!'

There was such a curious expression in Tyler's eyes that her smile faded slightly. 'When do you want to meet?'

But his expression had shuttered abruptly and he was getting to his feet. 'You'd better sort things out with Alan first.'

'Are you sure?' she asked, puzzled. 'I haven't forgotten the terms of our deal.'

'I'm sure.'

'All right,' said Mary gratefully. 'Thanks. I must admit, it would be easier to concentrate then. Perhaps we could arrange a session in a couple of days?'

'Fine,' said Tyler, thinking that in a couple of days she might be back together with Alan. 'Ring Carol and make an appointment when you're free.'

'Ms Thomas is here for her two o'clock appointment.'

Tyler's heart lurched uncomfortably. He wasn't sure if he had been longing for this moment or dreading it. 'Thanks, Carol. I'll be out in a moment.'

Swallowing hard, he put down the phone. This was uncharted territory for him. He knew now what he wanted. It had meant admitting that he had made a mistake, which hadn't been easy for him to do, but this time he was absolutely sure, and a goal was always a reassuring thing to have in mind. Only this time, for the first time in his life, Tyler had absolutely no idea of his strategy, or whether he would be able to get what he wanted after all.

In the next few minutes, he would know.

Outside, in Carol's office, Mary was gently rocking the pushchair as she chatted to Carol. She was swathed in a tweedy blue coat and a gaudily striped scarf, and Tyler decided she looked a bit like a scruffy robin, all round and pink-cheeked and bright-eyed. She looked glowing, he thought heavily. Had she sorted things out with Alan?

She broke off as Tyler appeared, but Bea had spotted him at the same time and gave a cry of delight. Crouching by the pushchair, he offered her a finger and, as she grabbed it, the tight feeling that had gripped him ever since he had said goodbye to her eased a little.

He glanced up to see Carol watching him indulgently, while Mary quickly lowered her lashes before he could read her expression.

'Mum's busy this afternoon,' she said, 'so I had to bring her with me.'

'I don't mind,' said Tyler. 'It's nice to see her again.' And that was an understatement, he thought, looking at the little fist gripping his finger so firmly.

'I wondered if you'd mind if we took her for a

walk while we talked? She'll never stay in her push-chair in your office.'

He straightened. 'A walk sounds good to me.' He didn't want to hear Mary tell him about Alan in the office anyway. Carol would be able to see his face afterwards, and Tyler wasn't sure that he would be able to bear that.

'Have you got a coat?' said Mary, nodding at his shirtsleeves. 'It's cold out.'

'I'll be all right in my jacket.' Quickly buttoning his cuffs, Tyler retrieved it from the back of his chair and shrugged it on.

They took the lift down to the ground floor in silence and walked down to the river front, the pushchair juddering over the cobbles. A weak November sun was doing its best to brighten the day, but it was having little effect on the temperature and it was as cold as Mary had warned. She stopped to put Bea's gloves on, and Tyler was glad to shove his own hands in his pockets as they walked.

A chill wind was gusting along the river, ruffling the surface of the water and swirling the drifts of fallen leaves. Tyler was content to walk beside Mary and let himself look at her properly for the first time. Having admitted to himself at last how much he loved her, he had somehow imagined that she would look different now that the scales had fallen from his eyes, but she didn't. She looked just the same. She was just Mary. His throat tightened painfully as he watched her. It was difficult to believe that he had ever thought her ordinary. When had he realised just how beautiful she really was?

The silence lengthened, until Mary tripped over an uneven paving stone and broke the tension.

'I'm as clumsy as ever,' she said ruefully.

Tyler's arm had shot out to catch her instinctively, but the pushchair had stopped her from falling and he put his hand back in his pocket before he did anything stupid like taking one of Mary's.

'How did you get on with Alan?' he asked abruptly. It wasn't his business, but he had to know.

'It was all right,' said Mary. 'I thought it would be really emotional, but actually, when I saw him, I felt quite calm and we had a good talk. He told me how he'd felt when I left. He was very angry and bitter, he said, and he didn't really want to admit that it had happened, that's why he was so unpleasant about the money.'

She glanced at Tyler, walking grim-faced beside her. 'Why didn't you tell me it was you who made him come to an agreement about my share of the house?'

'I didn't do anything,' he said evasively. 'I just got my solicitors to give him a bit of a fright. I didn't think it was fair that you were in a position where I could blackmail you into accepting a job.'

Mary smiled. 'I'm not sure of the logic there, but

thank you anyway. Your intervention made Alan realise that he was going to have to do something if he did want me back.'

Great, thought Tyler, the old leaden feeling growing heavier by the second. Why had he interfered?

'So he *does* want you back?'

'He says that he does,' said Mary carefully. 'He says that he missed me, and that he made a mistake. He said that he wanted me to come home.'

'You're going back to London, then?' He looked straight ahead, not wanting to see her smile and nod.

'No,' said Mary, and Tyler stopped abruptly. 'London's not home anymore,' she explained when he stared at her. 'This is home.'

'But…what about Bea?'

'It's because of Bea that I'm staying. Alan is prepared to accept her to have me back, but she deserves better than being tolerated. I'm sure she'll want to get to know him later, and he did say he would acknowledge her and have her to visit when she's older, but he doesn't want to share in her day-to-day care.'

'His loss,' said Tyler, thinking of the feel of Bea on his lap, of her gummy smile and the tight feeling in his throat when she reached out her chubby arms to him.

Mary couldn't help smiling as she remembered his insistence that he wouldn't be a hands-on father.

'You've changed your tune,' she reminded him, and he looked straight at her.

'Yes,' he said, 'I have.'

The silence fizzed quietly for a moment before Tyler looked away.

'But what about you? You said that you loved Alan.'

'I did,' said Mary. 'I loved him terribly, but I don't anymore. I realised that when I saw him. He wasn't there for me when I needed him most, and I'm not sure I would ever be able to forget that. Besides—'

She stopped abruptly. She had been about to say, Besides, I'm in love with you, and how awkward would *that* have been? They were only meeting so that she could give Tyler advice on how to pursue his relationship with Fiona.

'Besides what?'

'Oh…only that it made me wonder whether I had ever truly loved him,' she improvised quickly. 'Alan was like a dream. He was the kind of person I wanted to be with, and he had the kind of life I longed to have, but we never had a truly equal relationship. He was older, more experienced, and I was dazzled by him. I'm not dazzled anymore.'

Her words flooded Tyler with relief. He didn't know if he could make Mary love him, but at least she hadn't chosen Alan. That was a start.

'So what are you going to do now?' he asked.

'What I was always going to do,' said Mary.

'Move into that flat, bring Bea up, make a new life for myself.'

Try to forget you. She kept that one to herself.

They had reached an empty bench, and she parked the pushchair so that Bea could look at the dogs trotting, scampering or snuffling past on their afternoon walks, their owners huddled into bulky jackets.

'Shall we sit down for a bit?' she suggested. 'Or are you too cold?'

Oddly, Tyler didn't feel the least bit cold. Just being next to her kept him warm. 'I'm fine,' he said.

'Fine...your favourite word,' she teased him as she sat down and pulled up the collar of her coat against the wind. The Scarborough train rattled over the bridge, and in the distance the towers of the Minster looked almost pink in the wintery afternoon sunshine.

It felt so good to be with Tyler again. Mary was happy to simply sit next to him and let the reassurance of his solid presence seep into her, and it was hard to remember that this was supposed to be a consultation.

'Tell me how things are going with Fiona,' she said, rousing herself. 'And don't say fine!'

'I won't do that,' said Tyler, 'because they're not fine. In fact, they're going very badly.'

'Badly?' She looked at him in dismay. 'Why, what's happened?'

'Nothing's happened,' he said. 'That's the point. There's been no spark. Fiona's a nice woman, but I don't know how to talk to her.'

'I've told you, you just have to talk to her the way you talk to me.'

'But she's not you,' said Tyler. 'And that's the problem. Nobody's ever going to be you. I rang Fiona after I'd seen you on Wednesday and cancelled our date.'

Mary was struggling to take in what he was saying. *She's not you*, he had said. 'What…what did she say?' she asked, although what she really wanted to know was what he meant by *Nobody's ever going to be you*.

'She was great about it. I think it was a relief to her too. She told me that she'd only agreed to go out with me because she wanted to make her ex jealous, so we were being equally stupid and refusing to acknowledge that we were both in love with someone else. She still loves her ex-boyfriend and, as for me,' said Tyler casually, 'well, I'm hopelessly in love with you.'

'With m-me?' stammered Mary.

'With you,' he confirmed. 'It turns out,' he said, 'that you're the one I want, Mary.'

Her heart was beating so fast that it was hard to breathe, but Mary couldn't let herself believe it yet. 'You don't want me,' she said shakily.

'Don't I?' Tyler turned on the bench to take her face

between his palms, and his smile made the last gasps of air evaporate from her lungs. 'I hate to contradict such an expert on relationships as yourself, Mary,' he said, 'but I think you're wrong about that. I think I'm going to have to show you just how wrong you are.'

He kissed her then, a long, slow, irresistible kiss that left Mary's head reeling and her body thrumming and exhilaration dancing and pirouetting along every vein, as she melted joyfully into him, winding her arms around his neck and kissing him back. The kiss deepened and deepened, so intense that Tyler's hands fell from her cheeks to unbutton her coat, pushing his hands beneath the heavy fabric to slide around her and pull her closer.

'Now tell me I don't want you,' he challenged her breathlessly when they broke apart for air at last, his hands still roaming possessively over her lush curves.

'But I'm nothing like your ideal woman,' said Mary, but in spite of her protest she didn't move away. Well, it was a cold day, and it was wonderfully warm with his arms around her. No point in wasting body warmth, was there?

'I know,' Tyler agreed. 'It's ironic, isn't it? I was so fixed on the idea of someone blonde and elegant and sophisticated that I nearly missed what was right in front of me.'

Tilting her face up, he looked down into shining grey eyes. 'I've missed you,' he said. 'I've missed you more than I can say. I hate going home because you're not there, and Bea's not there. It's not home anymore, it's just a place where you're not.'

He kissed her warm, lush mouth. 'I didn't even know I loved you when you left, Mary. I did everything I could to tell myself that I didn't. I'd never been in love before, and I didn't want to accept that it had happened to me at last, but when I came to see you in your office and you told me Alan was back in your life, I couldn't deny it any longer. It was as if a great black hole had opened up in front of me.' His mouth twisted at the memory. 'I thought I'd lost you before I'd had a chance to tell you what you meant to me.'

'Why didn't you say anything then?' asked Mary, remembering how his face had closed and, clinging closer, still hardly able to believe that he loved her after all.

'I knew you would want to see Alan first,' said Tyler. 'I thought you would choose him because he's Bea's father, and because I knew how much you'd loved him. I thought that I'd left it too late. It was my own fault for being too stupid to understand that I'd been falling in love with you right from the start.'

'You told me you didn't believe in love,' Mary reminded him.

'That's because I'd never been in love before. How was I to know what had hit me like a truck, turning

my life upside down and calling into question everything I used to be so sure of?' Tyler kissed her again,
very tenderly, on the lips. 'I know what love is now,'
he said. 'You were the one who taught me. You told
me exactly what it should be.'

'I did? What did I say?'

'You said that I needed to marry someone who
could light up my life and make me feel better just
by being near me. That's what you do to me,' he told
her. 'You're my rock, Mary. Without you, nothing
makes sense, and everything I used to think was so
important just seems worthless.'

Her arms tightened around him and he rested his
cheek against her hair, breathing in her fragrance, his
heart swelling at the feel of her. 'You told me I
shouldn't marry anyone unless I couldn't live
without them,' he said, his voice very deep and low.
'I can't live without you, Mary. I know you're not
blond and you're not elegant but you're *real*. Yes,
there are slimmer women out there, women who
are more graceful and elegant and better dressed, but
they're not you. None of them will make my heart
lift when I'm near them. None of them will make me
count the hours until I can go home and hold them
again. I never felt at home until I met you, Mary,' he
said. 'And home's not home without you and Bea.'

'Oh, Tyler…' said Mary tremulously. 'Tyler…'
Her heart was so full she didn't know where to
begin, and the tears were spilling out of her eyes.

'Mary!' Tyler tightened his arms around her. 'Don't cry.'

'I can't help it,' she said tearfully. 'I'm so happy.'

A smile that started deep in his eyes spread slowly over Tyler's face, and his expression made Mary fizzle with joyful anticipation. 'I've missed you too,' she said. 'Bea has too. We both love you,' she told him, and their lips met in a long, sweet kiss that dissolved the memories of the last miserable days and left them with an intoxicating glow of happiness.

'Tell me you'll marry me,' said Tyler urgently at last.

'What about your goal?' asked Mary mischievously. 'You wanted a wife and a family you could show off to your peers.'

'I'm going to have them,' he said, smiling. 'I'm going to have a wife I adore and who loves me, and a beautiful daughter… Who wouldn't envy me? No, I've got a new goal,' he said confidently.

'Oh?' she said. 'What's that?'

The smile faded from his eyes and his expression was very serious as he looked into her eyes. 'To make you happy,' he said simply. 'To love you for the rest of my life.'

Mary blinked back the tears that were shimmering on the end of her lashes. 'That sounds like a pretty good goal to me,' she said.

'I'll need some help on my strategy, though,' he said. 'You know I'm not very good at relationships.'

She laughed a little shakily. 'Obviously, you're going to need some intensive coaching to make sure you get it right,' she agreed.

'That's what I thought,' said Tyler. 'I was hoping I could persuade you to take on that role.'

'Persuasion, not blackmail?' Mary applauded. 'Very good!'

His smile deepened. 'Do you think you'd be prepared to take it on?'

'Well…' She pretended to consider. 'It would take a very long time. We'd have to make it longer than a two month contract.'

'What sort of time scale are you thinking of?'

'A lifetime would be best,' said Mary, her lips curving into a smile as she kissed the corner of his mouth. 'Just to be sure. We'll both have to work at it, and we'll learn from each other, but as long as we look after each other, we'll get there.'

Tyler smiled. 'Sounds like a good strategy to me,' he said, and kissed her again, a kiss that went on and on until Bea realised that she had lost their attention and objected with a shout.

Laughing, Mary lifted her out of the pushchair and sat her on her knee. 'What do you think, Bea?' she asked. 'Shall we go back and live with Tyler and let him change your nappies?'

Tyler grinned. 'I'll even do that if it means you'll come home!'

'Gosh, you *have* missed us!'

'I have,' he said, suddenly serious. 'I never want to miss you like that again.'

'You won't need to,' said Mary softly. 'We'll all be together from now on.'

Bea was straining to get to Tyler and he took her from Mary, holding her out at arm's length and jumping her up and down on his knee while she dimpled and smiled and flirted her lashes at him, delighted to have his undivided attention once more.

'It looks like you've got the deciding vote, Bea,' he said. 'Are you going to let me marry your mum and look after you?'

Bea bounced excitedly on his knee. 'Ga!' she shouted, and Tyler smiled, settling her on his knee and putting his other arm around Mary to draw her close.

'I'll take that as a yes,' he said.

* * * * *

Next month The Brides of Bella Lucia *saga
continues in*
Married Under the Mistletoe
by
Linda Goodnight

Daniel has just arrived in London, having discovered that his long-lost father is John Valentine. Now, at the exclusive Knightsbridge Bella Lucia restaurant, Daniel may have finally met his match in beautiful manager Stephanie Ellison—but does he have the power to break down Stephanie's barriers?

STEPHANIE SQUEEZED out yet another mop full of water and watched in dismay as more seeped from beneath the industrial-sized dishwasher. She'd called the plumber again about this a week ago and still he had yet to show up. Ordinarily, she'd have followed up and called someone else, but she'd had too many other problems on her mind. One, the money missing from the Bella Lucia accounts—something that, as restaurant manager, she would have to sort out soon.

Two, Daniel Stephens. Since the moment he'd arrived, the man had occupied her thoughts in the most uncomfortable way. Then he'd taken her on that picnic and she'd realized why. She liked him. His passion for Africa stirred her. His relentless pursuit of an incredibly lofty goal stirred her. Looking at him stirred her.

A voice that also stirred her broke through the sound of sloshing water. "Ahoy, mate. Permission to come aboard."

Stephanie looked up. All she could think was, *Ohmygosh. Ohmygosh.*

She'd known he was coming. She'd been expecting him. But she hadn't been expecting this.

Barefoot and shirtless, Daniel waded toward her in a pair of low slung jeans, a tool belt slung even lower on his trim hips.

Close your mouth, Stephanie. Mop, don't stare.

But she stared anyway.

Daniel Stephens, dark as sin, chest and shoulder muscles rippling, black hair still wet and carelessly slicked back from a pirate's forehead was almost enough to make her forget the reasons why she could not be interested in him. Almost.

Slim hips rolling, he sloshed through the quarter inch of water to the dishwasher. Dark hairs sprinkled his bare toes.

The sight made her shiver. When had she ever paid any attention to a man's toes?

"You forgot your shirt," she blurted, repeating the slogan seen everywhere in American restaurants. "No shirt, no shoes, no service."

He grinned at her, unrepentant. "You said you needed me. *Badly*. How could I not respond immediately to that kind of plea from a beautiful woman?"

He thought she was beautiful? The idea stunned her. Beautiful? Something inside her shriveled. How little he knew about the real her.

He, on the other hand, was hot. And he knew it.

"Are you going to fix that thing or annoy me?"

One corner of his mouth twitched. "Both, I imagine."

He hunkered down in front of the washer, tool belt dragging the waist of his jeans lower. Stephanie tried not to look.

"Do you think it's bad?"

"Probably have to shut down the restaurant for a week."

Stephanie dropped the mop. It clattered to the floor. "You've got to be kidding!"

He twisted around on those sexy bare toes and said, "I am. It's probably a leaky hose."

"Can you fix it?"

He smirked. "Of course."

"Then I really am going to fire that plumber."

"Go ahead and sack the useless lout. Tell him you have an engineer around to do your midnight bidding."

Now, *that* was an intriguing thought.

She retrieved the mop. "Which is more expensive? A plumber or an engineer?"

White teeth flashed. "Depends on what you use for payment."

Time to shut up, Stephanie, before you get in too deep. Do not respond to that tempting innuendo.

Metal scraped against tile as he easily manhandled the large machine, walking it away from the cabinet to look inside and behind. Stephanie went back to swabbing the decks. Watching Daniel, all muscled and half naked, was too dangerous. Thinking about that cryptic payment remark was even more so.

"Could you lend a hand over here?" he asked.

Oh dear.

The floor, dangerously slick but no longer at flood stage, proved to be an adventure. But she slip-slid her way across to where Daniel bent over, peering into the back of the machine.

"What can I do?"

"See this space?"

Seeing required Stephanie to move so close to Daniel that his warm, soap-scented and very nude skin brushed against her. Thankful for long sleeves, she swallowed hard and tried to focus on the space in question.

"Down there where that black thing is?" she asked.

"Your hands are small enough, I think, to loosen that screw. Do you see it?"

"I think so." She leaned farther into the machine, almost lying across the top. Daniel's warm purr directed her, too close to her ear, but necessary to get the job done.

"That's it. Good girl."

His praise pleased her, silly as that seemed.

He pressed in closer, trying to reach the now un-fastened hose. His breath puffed deliciously against the side of her neck. Stephanie shivered and gave up trying to ignore the sensation.

Their fingers touched, deep inside the machine. Both of them stilled.

Her pulse escalating to staccato, Stephanie's blood hummed. As if someone else controlled her actions, she turned her head and came face to face with searing blue eyes that surely saw to her deepest secrets.

She needed to move, to get out of this situation and put space between them. But she was trapped between the machine, the hose, and Daniel's inviting, compelling body.

"I think I have it," she said, uselessly. Foolishly.

Daniel's nostrils flared. "Yes. You certainly do."

His lips spoke so close to hers that she almost felt kissed.

Daniel held her gaze for another long, pulsing moment in which Stephanie began to yearn for the touch of his lips against hers. How would they feel?

All right, she told herself. That's enough. Stop right now before you venture too close to the fire and get burned.

With the inner strength that had kept her going when life had been unspeakable, she withdrew her hand and stepped away.

As though the air between them hadn't throbbed like jungle drums, Daniel didn't bother to look up. He finished repairing the hose while Stephanie completed the mopping up and tried to analyze the situation. Daniel was interested in her. Big deal. In her business, she got hit on all the time.

But it wasn't Daniel's interest that bothered her so much. It was her own. Something in Daniel drew her, called to her like a Siren's song. One moment he was cynical and tough. The next he was giving and gentle. There was a strength in him, too, that said he could and would move a mountain if one was in his way. He was different from anyone she'd ever met.

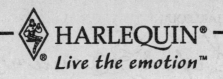

HARLEQUIN®
Live the emotion™

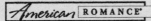

Heart, Home & Happiness

HARLEQUIN®
Blaze.
Red-hot reads.

Harlequin® Historical
Historical Romantic Adventure!

HARLEQUIN®

HARLEQUIN ROMANCE®
From the Heart, For the Heart

HARLEQUIN®
INTRIGUE®
Breathtaking Romantic Suspense

Medical Romance™...
love is just a heartbeat away

Next™

There's the life you planned.
And there's what comes next.

HARLEQUIN®

Seduction and Passion Guaranteed!

HARLEQUIN®
Super Romance®

Exciting, Emotional, Unexpected

www.eHarlequin.com   HDIR106

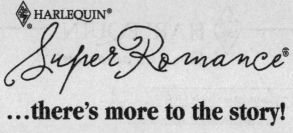

HARLEQUIN®
Super Romance®

...there's more to the story!

Superromance.
A *big* satisfying read about unforgettable
characters. Each month we offer *six* very different
stories that range from family drama to adventure
and mystery, from highly emotional stories to
romantic comedies—and much more! Stories
about people you'll believe in and care about.
Stories too compelling to put down....

Our authors are among today's *best* romance
writers. You'll find familiar names and talented
newcomers. Many of them are award winners—
and you'll see why!

If you want the biggest and best
in romance fiction, you'll get it
from Superromance!

Exciting, Emotional, Unexpected...

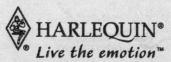

HARLEQUIN®
Live the emotion™

www.eHarlequin.com   HSDIR06

Harlequin® Historical
Historical Romantic Adventure!

Imagine a time of chivalrous
knights and unconventional ladies,
roguish rakes and impetuous
heiresses, rugged cowboys
and spirited frontierswomen—
these rich and vivid tales will
capture your imagination!

Harlequin Historical...
they're too good to miss!

www.eHarlequin.com   HHDIR06

SILHOUETTE *Romance*®

Escape to a place where a kiss is still a kiss...

Feel the breathless connection...

*Fall in love as though it were
the very first time...*

Experience the power of love!

Come to where favorite authors—such as

Diana Palmer, Judy Christenberry, Marie Ferrarella

*and many more—deliver modern fairy tale
romances and genuine emotion,
time after time after time....*

*Silhouette Romance—
from today to forever.*

Silhouette®
Live the possibilities

Visit Silhouette Books at www.eHarlequin.com.   SRDIR06

Silhouette

SPECIAL EDITION™

Emotional, compelling stories that capture the intensity of living, loving and creating a family in today's world.

Special Edition features bestselling authors such as Susan Mallery, Sherryl Woods, Christine Rimmer, Joan Elliott Pickart— and many more!

For a romantic, complex and emotional read, choose Silhouette Special Edition.

Silhouette®

Visit Silhouette Books at www.eHarlequin.com   SSEGEN06

HARLEQUIN®
Presents

The world's bestselling romance series...
The series that brings you your favorite authors,
month after month:

Helen Bianchin...Emma Darcy
Lynne Graham...Penny Jordan
Miranda Lee...Sandra Marton
Anne Mather...Carole Mortimer
Susan Napier...Michelle Reid

and many more uniquely talented authors!

Wealthy, powerful, gorgeous men...
Women who have feelings just like your own...
The stories you love, set in exotic, glamorous locations...

HARLEQUIN®
Presents

Seduction and Passion Guaranteed!

www.eHarlequin.com

HPDIR104

2 Love Inspired novels and 2 mystery gifts... Absolutely FREE!

Visit
www.LoveInspiredBooks.com

for your two FREE books, sent directly to you!

BONUS: Choose between regular print or our NEW larger print format!

There's no catch! You're under no obligation to buy anything. We charge nothing—ZERO—for your first shipment. And you don't have to make any minimum number of purchases.

You'll like the convenience of home delivery at our special discount prices, and you'll love your free subscription to Steeple Hill News, our members-only newsletter.

We hope that after receiving your free books, you'll want to remain a subscriber. But the choice is yours—to continue or cancel, anytime at all! So why not take us up on our invitation, with no risk of any kind!

LIGEN06